# Love Shouldn't Hurt 2

Lock Down Publications and Ca$h
Presents
# Love Shouldn't Hurt 2
A Novel by *Meesha*

Love Shouldn't Hurt 2

## Lock Down Publications

P.O. Box 870494
Mesquite, Tx 75187

**Visit our website @**
www.lockdownpublications.com

First Edition October 2018
Printed in the United States of America

*This is a work of fiction. Names, characters, places, and incidents either are products of the author's imagination or are used fictitiously. Any similarity to actual events or locales or persons, living or dead, is entirely coincidental.*

**Lock Down Publications**
**Like our page on Facebook: Lock Down Publications @**
www.facebook.com/lockdownpublications.ldp
Cover design and layout by: **Dynasty Cover Me**
Book interior design by: **Shawn Walker**
Edited by: **Tisha Andrews**

# Stay Connected with Us!

Text **LOCKDOWN** to 22828 to stay up-to-date with new releases,
sneak peaks, contests and more…
Thank you.

# Submission Guideline.

Submit the first three chapters of your completed manuscript to ldpsubmissions@gmail.com, subject line: Your book's title. The manuscript must be in a .doc file and sent as an attachment. Document should be in Times New Roman, double spaced and in size 12 font. Also, provide your synopsis and full contact information. If sending multiple submissions, they must each be in a separate email.

Have a story but no way to send it electronically? You can still submit to LDP/Ca$h Presents. Send in the first three chapters, written or typed, of your completed manuscript to:

LDP: Submissions Dept
Po Box 870494
Mesquite, Tx 75187

*DO NOT send original manuscript. Must be a duplicate.*

Provide your synopsis and a cover letter containing your full contact information.

Thanks for considering LDP and Ca$h Presents.

# Chapter 1
## Dot

My right hand to God, the plans I had that day were to go out and get something to eat with my friend Stan. The endless pasta from Olive Garden was calling my name in my sleep. We were walking across the parking lot and who the fuck did I see? Jonathan and my stupid ass daughter. Seeing them together after I told her ass the night before that he wasn't shit, made me hotter than fried chicken. Before I knew it, I was walking in their direction.

"Ain't this a bitch! This nigga been missing in action your whole muthafuckin' life and now he gets to play daddy! Bitch, I told you that every time I saw you I was gon' whoop yo' ass! I guess you figured I was playing."

They thought they were going to get to the truck before I could confront them, but it didn't quite work out for them. They were walking hand in hand like that nigga been in her life from the beginning. Picking up speed, I was damn near running toward them. Stan grabbed my arm trying to stop me from approaching them. I snatched away from his grasp and punched his ass in the chest to get him off me.

"Dot, take that shit down a notch and gon' about yo' business. If you think I'm about to stand here while you try to fight my daughter, you must be crazy as hell. You better take yo' ass in there and feed that homeless nigga that you're with," Jonathan said, pushing Kaymee toward the truck.

I didn't know why he was trying to push her ass to safety, but I wasn't trying to hear what he was talking about. This nigga made my life a living hell and it was all because of her bitch ass. If I didn't get pregnant with her, I would've still had my man. He made me suffer by forcing me to take care of a baby by myself. Well, he was going to suffer with blood. The shit he said only made my ears burn. All of a sudden, she was his daughter.

"Nigga, you would want to shut the fuck up talking to me. You can't come back into her life after all these years to play daddy. I took care of her when you didn't. You can't tell me how to discipline her!" I yelled.

"She is grown, Dot! You can't discipline her! The things I heard from her and even from your own mouth, all you've been doing is putting your hands on her. That shit is not happening as long as I'm around! I'll die for mine. Baby, get in the truck," he said, turning his head to address her.

His ass didn't know he had made his own death request. Didn't he know the saying, "Ask and you shall receive?" I pulled my 9-millimeter glock from my purse and aimed it at him. His precious Kaymee came running from behind the truck screaming for him to watch out as an evil grin appeared on my face. I didn't hesitate when I pulled the trigger, shooting her. I let another round off popping his ass, too. I didn't feel any remorse shooting my own child. *Don't fuck with me*, was all I thought as I lowered my piece.

"Dot, what the fuck did you do? I told you to leave that shit alone, but you never listen!" Stan screamed in my face.

I tuned Stan's words out while staring at both of them lying on the pavement. When I looked up, there were people coming out to see what was going on. I saw some with phones up to their ears, so I knew they were calling the law. Putting the gun back in my purse, I backed up and hauled ass back to the car. Stan was right behind me.

Almost to the car, I heard someone yell out, "Stop them! Don't let them get away!" By that time, we were in the car. Stan cranked it up and backed up without looking. A guy was trying to prevent us from leaving by standing behind the car as he slammed on the brakes. I looked at Stan, then back at the guy.

"Run his ass over!" I yelled. He stalled until I screamed in his face, "Run his ass over, nigga!"

Stan pressed on the gas and the guy had to dive to get out of the way. Speeding out of the parking lot, he almost collided with an SUV. Luckily for us, the driver swerved into the next lane, avoiding the impact while laying on their horn. Stan gained control of the car and took off doing about a hundred on the street until we got to the expressway. He was looking around for the police but there weren't any in sight. The sweat that poured down his face was an indication that he was nervous as hell. Me, I didn't give a fuck.

"Why the fuck would you shoot them in broad daylight like that, Dot? That was your muthafuckin' daughter! She did not deserve that shit! You made her pay for something that nigga did to you before she was born. That was foul, man!" he yelled, hitting the steering wheel.

"Check this out, nigga, I don't give a fuck how you feeling right now. That shit needed to be done. I told her muthafuckin' ass that I was gonna fuck her up on sight. She should've taken heed to that shit and went to the truck like her bitch ass daddy told her to. Instead, she wanted to come back and save a nigga that ain't did nothing for her! That bullet was for his ass, but since she put herself in the equation, I had one for her ass, too. Now drive this muthafucka so we can get rid of it. The police will be looking for this car."

He didn't say anything as he continued to drive. Every time I looked over to glance his way, he was shaking his head. I could've sworn I saw a tear fall from his eye, but I wasn't sure. I wish his pussy ass would cry, I would push his ass out of this bitch. Niggas always wanted to be about that life but scary as hell when they had to put in the work.

"Do you even care if she's hurt badly, Dot?" he asked after a while.

"To be honest, I hope the bitch ain't breathing! Why the fuck do you care, Stan? Don't say shit else to me with yo' punk ass. And you better not utter a word to nobody! This shit never happened. I want you to take this bitch to the abandoned warehouse on Halsted and put a match to this muthafucka. We will walk back to the hood, got it?" I said sternly.

# Meesha

## Chapter 2
### Montez

After Kaymee and Jonathan left, I went in the bedroom and turned on my Xbox. I usually didn't have time to fuck with it, but I was making time that evening. I had so much on my mind since seeing Mena. When she said my damn name, I got lost in her voice and it didn't make things better when she walked up to me and hugged me tightly. I didn't think twice about hugging her back. She felt as good as I remembered and I had no intentions of letting her go.

When Poetry said, "Um, excuse me", I knew I had fucked up. I moved away from Mena with the quickness, but I felt the tension in Poetry's body when I grabbed her around her waist. I introduced them to one another, but the look on Mena's face was one that I'd seen before. She was about to be on some bullshit. It wasn't like she didn't know I had a woman, she just didn't know shit about her other than her name.

G saved a nigga that night when he came down from his office. Mena made shit real obvious when she went behind the counter slamming shit around. It took G to shoot her the look of death for her to chill the fuck out. I felt Poetry staring at my face the entire time but she didn't speak on it. I was kind of relieved that she didn't, though, because I didn't feel like arguing with her.

I've known Mena for years and been fucking with her on a sexual level for about two. She knew what the fuck it was from the start but I guess seeing Poe made her feel some kind of way. That was on her, though. I didn't tell her to catch feelings for a nigga. What we had was pure sex—nothing more, nothing less.

She had been texting me since that day and I've been able to get away with it thus far. I didn't know how much longer I was going to be able to hold her off. She wanted the dick and she was getting aggressive with it. I'd been making excuses as to why I couldn't meet up with her. She wasn't the only one that wanted to meet up. I did too, but that shit would be suspicious as fuck with what happened at the club.

Poetry walked in, interrupting my thoughts. I looked up and started up my game of *Call of Duty*. I was still kind of mad at her for teasing Kaymee about what we heard the night before between her and Dray. That shit she did was childish as hell and I let her know it, too. She tried to argue her point and I wasn't trying to hear the shit.

"You about to play the game instead of chillin' with me? That only tells me you're still mad about earlier. I don't know why it upset you so much, but not Kaymee," she said, standing in front of me.

"Poe, I'm not mad. We already discussed the bullshit you pulled. It's over. Now get from in front of the TV," I said, trying to look around her.

When she moved, she walked to the door and closed it. She came back to the bed and started taking her clothes off seductively. Removing her shirt slowly, I tried not to pay her any attention because she always pulled this shit when I turned the game on. Looking out of the corner of my eye, she bent over with her back facing me and removed the shorts she was wearing. My joint swelled up instantly, her pussy looked good as hell from the back.

I fucked around and got gunned up because the game was playing itself. I wasn't paying attention to that muthafucka. She then reached between her legs and ran her hand along her lower lips. Biting my lip, I was fighting the urge to reach out and squeeze her ass. I was mesmerized and couldn't tear my eyes away from the sight before me. I threw the controller on the bed and got down on my knees. I crawled over to her and rubbed up and down her legs.

As I molded both of her ass cheeks with my hands, I moved my head forward to run my tongue along her clit. My phone started blaring Jay Z's, "The Take Over", and I held my head down while grabbing my cell off my hip. That was the ringtone indicating G was on the other end. There was no ignoring that call. That's how I ate.

Getting up, I sat on the bed and answered. "What up, boss?"

Poetry stood up straight and the irritation on her face couldn't be missed. She was pissed, snatching her clothes up and putting them back on a lot faster than she got out of them. I knew I had to make it up to her later.

"Yo, I need you to come to the Dungeon. I want to run some shit by you. I want to have the meeting before the end of the month since you will be leaving in a couple of weeks. Bring Dray with you. We can meet in about an hour. I have to get in touch with that nigga Jonathan, too."

"I saw him earlier. He went out with Kaymee to get to know her. They've been gone for a little minute but hit him up," I told him.

"That's good shit. I'm glad she agreed to meet up with him, but I'll see you niggas in a minute."

"Bet," I said, disconnecting the call.

I looked at Poe and she was pissed. Shit I was, too. There was no time to shower, get dressed, and get in them guts. She had to wait. The news wasn't going to sit well with her but shit, money was calling. Walking over to her, I tried to kiss her on the lips, but she turned her head.

"Come on, Poe. You know I gotta get this money. I'm sorry, baby. I'll make it up to you tonight," I said, staring into her eyes.

She didn't bother to respond. She crawled under the covers and turned her back on me. That's the childish shit I be talking about. She could have an attitude by her damn self. I wasn't about to entertain her. I grabbed a pair of jean shorts, a black tee, and pulled my black Huaraches from the box. Walking to the other side of the room, I opened the dresser and took out a pair of boxers and socks, leaving her ass lying right there as I headed to the shower.

I placed my clothes on the sink and went to tell Dray the plans. The door to his room was closed, so I knocked. He opened the door and the nigga was standing there looking like a bodybuilder, all oiled up and shit. Since Mee started coming over with his ass, he had been using coconut oil and shit.

"Damn, yo' black ass glistening and shit, nigga. Looking like a female around this bitch. Shit, you smell like one, too," I said, laughing at his ass.

"Fuck you. What yo' ass want?" he said, not finding what I said funny.

"We got to go meet up with G. We have less than an hour to get there so get yo' ass ready," I said, walking back to the bathroom.

"Why do he want me there? I'm not part of y'all squad."

"You are about to get put on. I told G how you've been helping a nigga get the product off. The dynamics of the operation will be explained in about an hour. Just get ready so we can roll out," I said over my shoulder as I walked down the hall to the bathroom.

It didn't take me no time to hop in the shower and throw my clothes on. It didn't take all that pampering for me to still look good just to hang around other niggas. That shit was for females anyway. I saved brushing my teeth as the last thing I did before putting on my shirt. Brushing my hair, I looked in the mirror and a nigga was ready to ride.

I grabbed the clothes that I took off and threw them in the hamper, letting the steam follow me out the door. When I got back to the bedroom, Poetry was still laying in the same spot with her head under the cover. I walked to the dresser and picked up my platinum chain, putting it over my head. I glanced over at the bed and decided to go show my baby some love.

Bending down, I pulled the cover back and kissed her on her cheek. "I'm about to be out. I'll be back later. I love you." I stood there waiting for her to respond. When she didn't, I shrugged the shit off and left out of the room. Dray was coming

16

out of his room as I grabbed my keys off the hook by the door and we left.

"You riding with me, fam?" I asked him, hitting the button to unlock my doors.

"Nah, I'm gonna ride solo. I'll tail you. I don't feel like listening to you bitching about me touching yo' radio. I want to listen to what I want," he said, walking to his rental.

"That's cool, too, nigga. Keep up," I said, smirking at him.

I hopped in my ride and hooked my phone to the Bluetooth after I started my car. I put on Jeezy radio and backed out of the driveway with Dray right behind me. Cruising down the street, I made sure to do the speed limit. I didn't want the pigs to have an excuse to fuck with me. It was another story when I hit the expressway, though. I pushed that bitch to the limit. That was the reason I purchased a Charger.

Dray was in the lane next to me trying to race. I looked over at him quickly and pushed down on the gas. I left his ass in the dust, laughing as I weaved in and out of traffic. Slowing down after about fifteen minutes, I let his slow driving ass catch up. I turned on my signal and checked the side mirror before merging over.

Getting off the expressway, I turned right at the light. Making my way to the Dungeon, I pulled into a spot and cut the engine. Dray whipped his ride next to me and got out. I hadn't been to this spot in a minute and it felt good to be back.

"You drive like you a Nascar racer. You better be lucky there weren't no police out."

"Man, fuck the police. You need to get yo' driving skills up to par if yo' ass wanna keep up with me," I said, laughing.

We walked up to the door and I rapped on it four times and waited. One of the Goons peeked out of the peephole and started unlocking the door. When it opened, Scony stood before me with a smirk on his face. I knew he had some slick shit on his tongue before he even opened his mouth.

"What's up, Similac! Good to see yo' ass again," he said, laughing.

I hated when he called me that shit. I was about the young-
est nigga on the Squad and that's where that shit stemmed
from, but I let it slide. I walked inside, bumping him hard as I
continued along. He stumbled a bit and I shot him a look over
my shoulder with a grin. "Get ya weight up, old man. I almost
ran ya ass over," I said, laughing right back at his ass.

"You better watch that shit, young buck," he threw back as
he locked the door. "Everybody is in the Blood Room," he
called out to my back.

As I made my way to the back of the Dungeon, I noticed
Dray looking around taking everything in. I could tell he had
questions, so I slowed down my pace just in case he wanted
some answers. So much shit had happened in this building that
the only way anybody knew the details was if they were part
of the Squad.

"What the fuck is the Blood Room?" he finally asked.

"It's whatever you think it is, fam. You will get the opportunity to ask any questions that you have in this meeting. I am
not at liberty to tell you what that means at this time. To know
the ins and outs of the operation, you first have to become a
Goon. Are you ready for that?"

Dray was about to answer the question when Scony
walked up behind us, draping his arms over both our shoulders.

"Good answer, Similac," he said, looking Dray in the face.
"If you ain't ready, you better make that shit known before you
hear anything that's about to be said in this muthafucka. It
wouldn't be in your best interest to make your decision after
the fact because you won't live to walk the streets again. Now,
I'm gon' ask you. Are you ready for this shit?"

Dray stopped walking and stared at Scony in the eyes and
said, "I was born ready."

"That's what the fuck I'm talking about! Let's get in here
because you niggas already late," he said, leading the way.

The Blood Room was a big ass open space that had chains
and hooks hanging from the ceiling. It smelled like bleach and
other chemicals that were used to get the smell of death out of

18

the building. The shit was strong as fuck. The ventilation system was on full blast, so we wouldn't die in that bitch. I knew right then a muthafucka stopped breathing in that very room not long ago.

"What up, Montez, Dray. Glad y'all could make it," G said from the center of the room.

"What's up, G. I had to keep slowing down so this nigga could keep up with me on the road. You already know I left his ass in my exhaust smoke." Everybody started laughing at my joke

"Hey, man. It's good to see you again. I wanted to thank you again for all you've done," Dray said, stepping to G and shaking his hand.

"No problem, Dray. It's all good."

There were about thirty niggas standing around waiting for the meeting to start. As I scanned the room, I noticed that Jonathan wasn't amongst them. I didn't think anything of it and waited for G to start the meeting.

"Okay, I think we can start this shit so we can get the fuck out of here. Y'all know how the wifey gets when I'm away from the home front too long. I tried hitting that nigga Jonathan up, but he ain't responding. I'm gonna give that nigga a pass since he is out spending much needed time with his daughter."

G looked around the room and cleared his throat before continuing what he had to say. "The Goon Squad is a family and I wanted all of you here to help me swear in a new member. This nigga came with high recommendations from Montez. I think I want to give the lil' nigga a chance. I was told that his gunplay ain't no joke and his hustle is on point, too. He has been helping Montez move the product in Atlanta without hesitation and he's getting rid of that shit faster than a candy lady in the projects. If the two of them are moving shit like that off one nigga's load, just imagine what the fuck they can do if we doubled the shit. Well, that's what's about to happen," he said, turning to Dray.

"I like the way you move, homie. I need to know if you ready to be in this shit for the long haul and make this mutha-fuckin' money. There won't be no quitting. You better think about the shit before you commit."

Dray didn't need time to think anything over because his mind was already made up. "Like I told Scony when we were walking to this room, I was born ready. I see the way brah breaks me off and is still getting money hand over fist, so I want in. Not to mention, Goon Squad got a nice ring to it," he said, smiling.

"A'ight, that's what's up. From this point on, you are declared a member of the Goon Squad. Anything we say amongst the family, stays amongst the family. When I eat, you eat. It doesn't pay to take what don't rightfully belong to you. If there's a leak within the circle, the nigga responsible will be taken care of accordingly. That means that person will no longer breathe on this earth. We don't tolerate snakes of any kind, so it would be wise for you to stay loyal because there isn't anyone in this room that would think twice about shooting you between the eyes. Ya boy, Montez, included. Do you agree to the terms of the Squad, Dray?"

"I agree," he said, rubbing his hands together.

"There you have it. Welcome to the Goon Squad. Meeting adjoined, muthafuckas. I'll get back up with y'all after I talk to Jonathan. Definitely before y'all head back down south. I got some pussy that's waiting on me and she done texted me thirty damn times already," G said, walking out the room.

As I said my goodbyes, my phone buzzed. I took it off my hip and looked down at it. Placing my thumb on the home button, my phone unlocked. There was a picture message from Mena. I stared at the unopened text, contemplating if I should open it or not. I didn't use my better judgment and pressed on it.

"You ready to roll, fam?" Dray asked as I opened the message.

The image popped up and I walked away from him. Mena had taken a pic of her pussy. That muthafucka was pretty too. The way it glistened told me that she had been playing all in her snatch. My dick bricked up the minute I saw it, and the caption didn't make it no better.

**Mena: Cum lick her clean, Zaddy.**

The message ended with a kissy face emoji. I knew I needed to take my ass home to Poetry, but my dick had other plans. The way her sugary walls felt around my shit was vividly in my mind and I needed that fix. My mind was already made up and there was no turning back. I looked over my shoulder at Dray and said, "Nah, go 'head. I got something to handle real quick." Then I headed for the door.

***

Walking briskly to my ride, I popped the locks and jumped in. I waited until Dray pulled off before I made my way further south, heading to Mena's crib. I texted her while I was driving, letting her know I was on my way. She only lived about fifteen minutes from the Dungeon and it didn't take no time to pull up to her spot.

As I cut off the engine, her door opened and she stood there in nothing but the skin she was born in. I looked around to make sure no one was out and about to see her freaky ass. The long strides I took got me to the door in record time. I pushed her back as I made entry into the house. Kicking the door close with my foot, I reached behind me and locked it, never taking my eyes off her frame.

Mena was stacked and what I meant by that, baby girl had titties, a small waist, and a humongous ass to go with it. I grabbed her around the waist as I lowered my head to kiss her lips. She didn't waste no time unbuckling my belt. Our tongues were wrestling sloppily, as my hands palmed her ass. She was having a hard time with the button on my shorts. If she wanted to get the hidden treasure, she had to work for it.

I removed my left hand from her ass and grasped her breast. I broke the kiss and took her breast into my mouth. I ran my tongue over her protruding nipple and sucked on it like a baby nursing. Nibbling on it softly, I gripped her breast and sucked on it a little harder.

"Sss, mmm," she moaned.

Moving my hand from her ass, I slid my finger down the crack of her ass and slowly inserted my middle finger in her back door. She took a deep breath and arched her back, throwing her ass back on my finger. My joint jumped and pressed against my zipper. It was trying to fight its way out on its own. I let go of her breast and freed Willy because that shit was painful.

Walking her backwards toward her sofa, I removed my finger from her ass when her back connected with it. I hoisted her up until her head was on the cushions and her twat was in the air. My mouth started watering and I dropped to my knees. I pulled my shirt over my head and threw it behind me. Running my tongue up and down her clit, I covered it with my lips and sucked hard. Her sweet nectar coated my tongue and it tasted like pineapples.

"Oh fuck! Eat that shit, Montez!" she screamed, while clawing at my scalp.

I used both of my forefingers to spread her juicy lips apart. Her clit peeked out and it was swollen. Her kitty was pink and looked like sugary cotton candy. I wanted her sweetness to invade my taste buds. Flicking my tongue against her nub rapidly, I covered her entire kitty with my mouth. While I sucked, I stuck my tongue deep inside her wet tunnel. Her walls closed down on my tongue and I couldn't move that muthafucka until she decided to release it.

"Mmmmm, uuughhh," she moaned, grinding against my mouth.

I went back to give her bud my undivided attention and attacked it fiercely. The way she was grinding, one would have thought she knew how to ride a horse, but I met her with every

22

stroke she thrusted my way. I held her hips in my hands and let her work.

"Oh, Montez! I'm about to cum!" she screamed.

Without responding verbally because I had her whole fatty in mouth, I continued to feast on it to get to her creamy center. She started bucking against my mouth harder, so I knew she was on the brink of letting go. I massaged the top of her pussy, which was one of her sexual spots and she bucked harder.

"I'm cummin', baby! I'm cummin'! Ugggghhh!" she yelled out as she squirted down my throat.

I used my tongue to flick her bud as all of her juices ran down my chin. She was panting fast, so I knew she was still in the mist of cummin'. I clamped down on her bud with my lips and sucked the soul out of her body. She started pushing my head so I would stop, but I wasn't having it. This is what the fuck she called me over here for. I finally released her clit and stood up. Moving back, my shorts fell to the floor and I stepped out of my shoes, kicking everything behind me.

"You ready for this dick, Mena?" I asked, stroking my pipe.

"Mmhmm."

She said that shit without opening her eyes. I looked down at her and she was trying to drift off to sleep. Not on my watch she wasn't. I came over here to fuck. There wasn't about to be no sleep in this muthafucka. I reached down and grabbed her shoulders, sitting her up on the back of the couch. Then I picked her up under her arms like a baby and she wrapped them around my neck. Her legs automatically wrapped around my waist. That was fine by me because I could get my pole in from that angle, too.

I lifted her up a bit and eased her ass on my joint. She moaned into my neck and I held her cheeks in both hands. Guiding her up and down on my shaft, her walls gripped me tightly. I picked up the tempo and my toes started to curl, digging deeply into the carpeted floor.

"Shit, girl! Grrrrr!" I growled.

23

The way her kitty suctioned my meat, it was hard for me to concentrate. Bending my knees, I bounced her up and down faster. The electrical current that I felt soaring through my body was one I had never felt before. I had to keep telling myself what was going on was just sex. With the type of pussy that she had, Mena could fuck up a nigga's whole understanding.

"Montez! Oouuuu! I'm cummin'!" she moaned loudly.

Mena's moans had me ready to let loose. I took rapid breaths to prolong my orgasm, but it didn't help. My balls felt as if they were ready to explode and that's exactly what they did. I lifted Mena's body up one last time before I spilled all of my babies on the back of her sofa.

"Grrrrrrr! Aaaaaaaah, damn!" I groaned out, while holding her tightly. I used all of the strength in my left arm to hold her, while I stroked my pipe with my right hand to release all my seeds.

My legs felt like noodles as I eased Mena to the floor before I collapsed. Falling on my shorts, I felt my phone vibrating. I took it from the clip and saw that I had a ton of missed calls and text messages from Poetry and Dray. I opened the first text and my heart dropped.

**Bae: Kaymee was shot! Why the fuck you not answering?**

I jumped up, grabbing my clothes. Heading to the bathroom, I took a quick shower and dressed quickly. I raced toward the door without saying anything to Mena. When I reached for the knob, she grabbed my arm stopping me.

"It's like that? You just gon' hit and leave?" she asked with hurt in her eyes.

"I gotta go, ma. I can't explain now, but it's not like that. I'll call you later," I said, opening the door and slamming it behind me.

## Chapter 3
### Poetry

I was sitting on the foot of Monty's bed watching *Black Ink Chicago* and eating ice cream. With Kaymee still out with Jonathan, I didn't have anything else to do. Monty's funky ass left me with a gushy twat and bounced. The shit had me deep in my feelings, too, but I ignored him until he left out the front door. I wasn't sleep. I just didn't want to be bothered with him after that.

"Man, Van stop bitchin', nigga! If y'all wasn't so messy, 9Mag would still be up and running. Ryan had to move around because y'all was holding him back!" I yelled at the TV like they could hear me.

Reality shows were fun and entertaining to watch, but much better when it was me, Kaymee and my mama talking shit together. Thinking of my mama, I picked up my phone and dialed her up. She answered on the third ring, sounding happy as ever.

"Hey, mama's baby! How are you?"

"I'm good, but I'm bored. What got you all chipper over there?"

"Girl, God is good! He opened my eyes this morning! I personally don't need a reason to be happy, Poetry. Life is too short to be moping around looking lost for whatever reason. You better get like me!" she said, laughing.

I loved my mama to death. She meant everything to me and she knew it, too. Hearing her voice always took my mind off whatever was bothering me.

"Well, alright nah. What are you up to over there?" I asked because I heard water running in the background.

"I'm cooking. You should come over for dinner. I'm making meatloaf, mashed potatoes, and corn. Tell Kaymee, Montez, and Dray they are welcomed to come. I've made more than enough. Plus, I want to thank you all for putting a smile on my baby's face last night. That's what friendship is about."

"They are all out doing their own thing, but I'll be there. I'm not turning down a good meal! Speaking of last night, y'all should've stayed!" I said, screaming in her ear as I snatched the bowl off the bed and headed to the kitchen.

"What the hell happened, Poetry? Don't tell me y'all was out in public drunk."

I could picture her now standing with her hands on her hips with a scowl on her face. She didn't play when it came to the two of us. Sometimes it was funny, but other times it could be scary.

"Nawl, it wasn't nothing like that. Dot came in showing her natural behind," I started before she cut me off.

"I thought she wasn't invited! How the hell did she find out about the party?" she yelled.

"She wasn't invited and it's still a mystery as of how she found out. Let me tell you what went down, ma. Stop cutting me off. Dot was screaming about how Kaymee wasn't about to have fun without her and she needed to come home. She tried to drag Kaymee out by her arm and sis snatched away. Dot slapped her then started beating her in the head. A guy came up to Dot and pulled her off of Kaymee. Come to find out, it was Kaymee's daddy!"

I was ecstatic that my girl had another parent other than her evil ass mama. I was praying for her and Jonathan to build a relationship. She needed someone in her life to love her. I meant the kind of love that one could only get from a mother or a father. She needed to experience that type of love and I believed it was going to come straight from Jonathan.

"Wait a damn minute, Poetry! Her daddy? Where the hell did he come from? Better yet, where has he been all this time? Let me sit down. You done called and spilled all the tea!"

"Yeah, Dot was saying a lot of sh— stuff that didn't leave room for speculations. Everything she said screamed, 'he's the daddy'. She was acting as if Kaymee was creeping with her man or something. She even said every time she saw Kaymee, she was gonna beat her up. It was sad and I knew my bestie

26

was embarrassed. Dot had to be carried out of the club, that's how crazy she was acting. As far as her daddy goes, he was locked up for twelve years and has been looking for Kaymee for the last two years."

My mama didn't say anything for a few seconds. I had to look down at my phone to make sure the call hadn't dropped. She was too quiet, so I spoke into the phone, "Ma, you still there?"

"I'm still here. I had to take a breather to calm down. I wish I was there because her ass would've been carried out on a stretcher. It makes no sense at all how she treats that child. She's going to regret shit later on down the line. I hope he can bring some stability into her life. She needs someone to teach her about the things that she is clueless about. I also hope he will be there for the long haul and don't up and leave her high and dry. Where is Kaymee now?"

"She went out with Jonathan. He wanted to sit down and talk to her and she accepted the invitation. I think it was a good idea. I can't wait to hear how everything panned out.

"That's a start and I think it was big of her to hear him out. Let me get off this phone and finish dinner. I'll be seeing you in about an hour, right?"

"Yes, ma. I'll be there. I'm about to get myself ready and I'll see you in a minute. Love you."

"I love you, too," she said, ending the call.

I found myself going to my text messages. I went to Monty's name and opened it up. It hadn't been too long since he left, so I didn't really want to start texting him. I wanted to let him know I was stepping out. It was the right thing to do as his woman, so I started typing.

**Me: Hey, baby. I'm going over to moms for dinner. Just wanted you to know.**

I pressed the send button and went to the closet to select an outfit. I decided on a pair of skinny jeans and a green tie tee shirt. I loved that shirt because it showed off the two rose tattoos I had on my back. I walked over to the dresser, looked in

27

the mirror, and smiled. I was a beautiful dark-skinned sista, one that loved everything about myself.

Picking up the comb, I started wrapping my hair in a circle. I grabbed my silk scarf and tied it over my hair. I snatched my clothes from the stool and walked out the bedroom to the shower. I laid my clothes on the counter and reached for my toothbrush to brush my teeth for the second time that day. After my mouth was squeaky clean, I leaned over and turned the knob for the shower to allow the water to heat up. Sitting on the toilet, I relieved my bladder because I had been holding my piss for the longest. I wiped myself and washed my hands at the sink.

Taking my shower cap off the hook, I put it on making sure my scarf was fully covered. I stepped into the shower and flipped the switch and the water sprayed over my body. Washing thoroughly with the mango scented body wash from Bath and Body Works. The muscles in my body relaxed and so did my mind. I shut the water off, stepped out, and grabbed the towel that I had lying on the sink. Wrapping the towel around my body, I took the shower cap off and shook it out before hanging it back up.

I dried off, applied coconut oil over my body and put on my clothes. Settling on a little bit of eyeliner and colored lip gloss, I didn't feel like putting on a whole face. I was only going to my mom's. Gathering the clothes off the floor, I put them in the hamper and went to the bedroom.

Walking into the bedroom, I automatically walked to the bed picking up my phone. When I looked down at the screen and there wasn't a notification indicating I had a text, or even a missed call, I was pissed. I sent that text to Monty over thirty minutes prior. Opening the phone, I went back to the original text and the nigga didn't even look at it.

Maybe I was overreacting and he was taking care of business. "He better hoped that was all the fuck was going on," I said to myself as I put on my low top Chucks. I went to the Lyft app on my phone and requested a ride.

\*\*\*

I pulled up to my house thirty minutes later. "Thank you," I said to the driver. He turned around watching me get out of his car. As I was closing the door he called out to me, I acted like I didn't hear him and let the door closed. Walking up the driveway, I heard the car door close.

"Aye, lil' ma. Can I talk to you for a minute?" he called out.

Sighing long and hard, I didn't turn around right away because this negro had fifteen minutes to shoot his shot. He didn't know that I wasn't interested, but he was about to find out. I pivoted so I would be facing him and he started walking up. He didn't have to do all that The conversation wasn't going to last long at all.

"What's up?" I asked, avoiding eye contact.

"I just wanted to tell you how beautiful you are. How can I get to know you?"

I was already on one because Monty still hadn't called or texted my phone. So, I really wasn't in the mood to entertain this dude. He was ugly anyway. I knew that I had to cut this shit short from the gate. I didn't need to get to know anyone because Monty was crazy.

"Thank you and getting to know me isn't possible. I have a whole man and ain't no new friends about to pop up out of the blue. That's one problem I'm not trying to deal with. Enjoy the rest of your night," I said, walking to the door.

He got the message because he walked back to his car and drove off. I inserted my key into the lock and entered the house. The aroma smacked me in the face and my stomach growled loudly. I went straight to the kitchen following the smell of greatness. My mama was sitting at the table already eating.

"Hey, pretty lady. You got it smelling good in here," I said, kissing her on her cheek. I looked around and didn't see my dad. "Where is daddy?'

"There's my baby. Your daddy went out with your Uncle Charles. They went to paint Shirley's damn kitchen. You know last month her son burned the damn kitchen down. She had to get it remodeled but they wanted to charge her an arm and leg to paint it. She told they ass to leave it alone," she said, shaking her head.

Shirley was my Uncle Charles wife, but he didn't claim her ass. He'd always say that it was cheaper to keep her and got a whole other family across town. He better hoped she didn't ever find out because all hell was going to break loose when the shit hit the fan. I wanted to be front and center when it went down though.

"Free is good. I don't blame her. Let me go in here and wash my hands so I can smash this food you cooked."

"Yeah, you better not go in my kitchen with your dirty ass hands. You're doing the right thing," she said, spooning some mashed potatoes in her mouth.

After washing my hands, I went straight to the kitchen and pile food on a plate. Saying a silent prayer, I cut a small piece of meatloaf and put it in my mouth after sitting down.

"Mmmm," I moaned, closing my eyes.

The seasoning in that gravy was on point. I almost had an orgasm it was so good. I felt my mama's eyes on me and I opened my left eye, peeking over at her.

"What?" I asked with a smirk on my face. I already knew she was about to talk shit about the noise I made. She hated it.

"You already know what, Poetry. Cut that shit out."

I picked up my phone and I snarled at it. Monty still hadn't called or texted me back. Forget texting his ass. I pushed the phone icon and called him. Biting down on my lip when he didn't answer, I called again and got the same results. Never have I ever had to call him more than once, but the feeling that came over me was not a good one. Call it a woman's intuition, but my mind was telling me this nigga was up to no good.

My appetite was completely gone at that point and all I wanted were answers. I wasn't trying to hear no kind of excuses because he wasn't working that damn hard that he didn't see me calling. I scrolled through my contacts and pressed Dray's name. The phone rang but he didn't answer either. The only thing that went through my mind was the bitch from the club. He'd better have a good reason as to why he wasn't answering.

"Is everything okay, baby?" my mama asked, taking a sip of water.

"Yes, it will be. Nothing to worry about," I said, placing my phone back on the table

Finishing my food while making small talk with my mama, I tried to keep my mind off Montez Watson. As I stood to take the plates to the kitchen, my mom's cellphone started ringing as I walked away. I heard her get up from the table and walk to her bedroom. She didn't come out right away and I could hear her talking lowly, as if she was trying to prevent me from hearing. Eavesdropping wasn't my thing, so I turned the water on in the sink and started washing the dishes.

Ten minutes or so later, my mom walked into the kitchen with a frown on her face. She stood there for a minute with her head lowered to her chest. When she lifted it back up, she had tears welling up in her eyes. Something bad had to have happened, but she hadn't said anything yet.

"Mom, what's going on?" I asked, walking toward her.

"We have to go, Poetry. That was the hospital on the phone. Kaymee was shot," she choked out.

Hearing my mom say the words, "Kaymee was shot", had me frozen in place. Once the words registered in my head, I felt my body giving way. I collapsed on my knees and started crying like a baby. The mere thought of losing my best friend was something that I couldn't handle.

"Please tell me she's okay! I can't lose her, ma. She's my best friend, my sister, my everything," I said, breaking down more.

My mom let me cry until I was hiccupping. My eyes felt as if I had a ton of sand in them, they were so dry. She helped me to my feet and I walked to the chair and grabbed my phone and purse. My mom went to her room and grabbed everything she needed. She walked briskly to the door and snatched the keys out of the glass bowl. I opened the door and went to the car while she locked up.

The ride to the hospital seemed like it took forever, but it was only a fifteen-minute commute. My mind was going wild because the only thing I could think about was my bestie getting shot. I stared at my phone and dreaded calling Monty. He was going to go ballistic when he heard about Kaymee.

I pressed his name and waited for him to answer. Instead of hearing his voice, I got the voicemail again. This wasn't the time for me to get mad about the other times I didn't get an answer, I had to keep trying for Kaymee. I dialed him several times in a row and I still got the same response, nothing. Finally, I gave up and left a text.

**Me: Kaymee was shot! Why the fuck you not answering?**

My mama pulled into the hospital parking garage because there weren't any parks on the street. We rushed out of the car and headed to the elevators. Going straight to the counter, my mama gave Kaymee's name. We were then directed to the floor she was on after getting our visitors' passes. She was in room 412 and I was nervous to go up.

"Baby, I want you to calm down. Kaymee is strong and I know she is going to be okay. You have to have faith and trust in the lord," my mama said, drawing me in for a hug.

"I know, ma, but I'm scared that she is badly hurt. I don't know what I would do without my best friend. I've never thought my friend would ever get shot. You hear about all the killings on the news and when it hits home, it doesn't feel good at all," I said, crying into her chest.

"Come on. Let's go see about my baby," she said, leading the way to the elevators.

The elevator stopped on the fourth floor and I stepped off. My mama walked over to the nurse's station and asked to speak to the doctor that was taking care of Kaymee. As the doctor was summoned, I turned to my mama and asked the one question that was on my mind.

"Ma, how did they know to call you about Kaymee?"

"That's the same question I asked when I got the call. I was told that I was listed as her emergency contact in case of an emergency. She must've changed it after she went to the hospital a couple weeks ago. I've been wondering if I should call Dot to let her know what's going on."

"I think we should wait until we know how Kaymee is doing. She may not be ready to talk to her after last night."

As I finished what I was saying, the doctor walked our way. He was the finest doctor I had ever seen in my life and he wasn't that old. That was not the time for me to be lusting over my best friend's doctor. Her condition should've been my main focus, but at that moment, it wasn't.

"The family of Kaymee Morrison?" he asked, leaning against the desk.

"Yes, that's us. How is she?" My mom asked.

He sighed and stood up straight. "Hello, I'm Dr. Reid. I'm the doctor that's assigned to Miss Morrison. She was shot in her forearm and was very lucky. It's very rare for one to endure a gunshot to the arm and not sustain severe damage. We took x-rays of her arm and there wasn't any muscle damage at all. The only problem that we saw was a fracture to her ratio bone. We cleaned the wound and bandaged it. The bone in her arm can't be set until the swelling around it goes down. Once that happens, hopefully in a day or two, we will stitch her arm and apply a cast. She is on an IV for fluids and antibiotics to prevent infections. With that being said, she is very healthy and will make a full recovery. You all can go in to see her. I'm quite sure she would be happy you're here."

Dr. Reid led us into the room and Kaymee was sleeping with her arm stretched out on the bed. I walked to the chair on the side of the end table and pulled it closer to her. As I looked at her, my nerves began to settle. I guess seeing she was all right was what I needed. She had to wake up soon because I was curious to know how this happened.

"Where is Jonathan?" I asked out loud.

"Yes, Dr. Reid? Was Kaymee the only person that was brought in from the scene?" my mama asked.

He rubbed his head without speaking and took a deep breath. "No, there was an older guy that was brought in, as well. I'm not permitted to give any information on his status. We haven't been able to reach a next of kin."

I fished around in my purse and took out my phone. I tried to get in contact with Monty for the hundredth time and still got his voicemail. Dray was the next person that I reached out to. Instead of calling, I sent a text. Maybe he didn't answer because he was trying to cover for his boy and didn't want to be in the middle of his bullshit.

**Poetry: Dray, I need you to get to Northwestern Memorial. Kaymee was shot. Call ya boy while you're at it because he's not answering me.**

A few seconds passed and he texted back.

**Dray: She was shot! How? I'm on my way.**

**Poetry: She's in room 412.**

I didn't bother to answer his question because I didn't know. Sitting back looking at my best friend, I thought about who I could call to tell about Jonathan. I knew he was the guy that was brought in with her. It had to be. Something was telling me that he would be right by her side in her time of need. They had just found out about each other and I'm sure he wouldn't leave her.

My mind went back to the planning of her surprise party and that's when I remembered that I had G's number. I scrolled through my text messages and found our thread. I got up to leave the room because I needed to smoke to get my mind right. G looked like the kind of guy that was going to go ape shit crazy when I told him about what happened.

"Where are you going, Poetry?" my mama asked.

"I'm going to call Jonathan's nephew. I know he was the one that was brought in with her. I'll be right back," I said, leaving out.

I went to the elevator and pressed the button to go downstairs. When the elevator came, I got on and pressed the button for the lobby. I rushed out of the elevator when the doors opened. I walked outside and went down the street to the park that wasn't too far away. Sitting down on a bench that was in the cut, I pulled out my weed and a blunt. Breaking down the blunt, I fed it well with the loud my mouth was watering for. Once I had licked and sealed it closed, I flamed up and took a deep pull.

Remembering the reason that I came outside, I picked the phone up from my lap and pressed the phone icon on G's name. He answered after a couple rings.

"What up, youngin'? The party planning is over. What is the reason for this call?" he asked in a deep baritone voice.

His voice had me stuck for a minute, but I shook it off. This was about Jonathan and Kaymee. Not me and my hot ass thoughts. "Um, I'm sorry to bother you. I didn't know who else to call. Kaymee and Jonathan went out today to get to know each other," I said.

"Yeah, I know about that. How did it go?"

"I don't know. My mom received a call saying that Kaymee was shot. She's fine but there was a guy brought in with her, but they won't tell us anything about him. I know it's Jonathan because if it wasn't, he would be here with my friend," I said, pulling on the blunt again.

"This explains why he wasn't answering my calls. What hospital are they in?" he asked a little too calmly for my liking.

"Northwestern Memorial is where we are. Kaymee is in room 412. Please stop in and tell me what's going on with him. Can you do me a favor? Call Monty and let him know what's going on. I've called and he hasn't responded."

"I got you. I'll keep you posted. I'm heading to the hospital now. Thanks for reaching out to me. I really appreciate that. A lot of people that have known me forever haven't put two and two together about Jonathan and me. Anyway, I'll hit that nigga Montez up, too. See you in a minute, ma. Keep ya head up. Everything will be all good."

He ended the call and I sat finishing my blunt. I was racking my brain trying to figure out what happened. The only thing that came to mind was a random act of violence. This had to be one of those incidents where they were caught in a crossfire. There couldn't be any other explanation. I was definitely ready to ask questions once Kaymee woke up.

As I stood to head back to the hospital, my phone rang. Looking down I saw it was my mom calling. I pressed the button to connect the call. "I'm on my way back now, ma," I said without saying hello.

"Good, because Kaymee is awake," she said, hanging up.

I flung my purse strap onto my shoulder, damn near running back to the hospital. I had to see for myself that she was doing good. Not only that, I needed to know what the hell happened.

## Chapter 4
### Drayton

After leaving the Dungeon, I headed straight to the house to think about the role I signed up for. It was true that I helped Monty get his shit off, but I didn't know if I was ready to tackle a load of my own. There wasn't anything that I couldn't do, but I was going to do my best to succeed. As I drove to Monty's crib, I couldn't wait to cuddle with Kaymee. I'd been thinking about her the entire time she'd been gone. A smile instantly appeared on my face when I pulled into the driveway.

I thought my baby girl would've been back from spending time with her pops, but the house was quiet and dark when I stepped inside. I turned on the lamp by the door so I could get to my room without knocking anything over. She hadn't called nor texted and I didn't want to bother her, but it had been hours since I'd talked to her. I had been thinking about the way she tasted all day. She had a nigga's nose wide open. I couldn't lie, I was missing her ass.

Walking to the bedroom, I sat on the side of the bed with my phone in hand. I was contemplating if I should call or not. As I thought it over, I decided to make the call. When she didn't answer, I felt as if I wasn't her priority at that moment. She was trying to get to know her father and I wasn't going to interrupt that union by constantly calling.

Glancing down at my watch, I noticed that the baseball game was about to start. The *Chicago Cubs* were playing the *St. Louis Cardinals*. That would occupy my mind until she came in. I took off my shoes, sat in the middle of the bed, and grabbed the remote. Once I was comfortable, I turned to the game and Marcell Ozuna hit a homerun to start the game. The Cubs were going to lose this one because I was with the Cardinals all day.

The end of the third inning went by fast as hell and just as I thought, the Cardinals were getting in that ass. My mind drifted to Monty. I assumed he took Poetry out for the night.

She had called me earlier after I left the meeting, but I didn't answer because I didn't know where he was headed. But she never called again and I didn't think anything else about it. He was in his phone like he had major plans set in place. I didn't ask him anything further than if he was ready to roll. That's what I wanted to be on, spending time with Kaymee.

She was so innocent but she had been through so much with her crazy ass mama. I had plans to make her forget how she was treated growing up. I couldn't imagine either of my parents treating me the way that her mom did her. I would've left and never looked back. I'm glad Jonathan finally found his way back to her. He had valid reasons as to why he was absent from her life, but he was back now.

I didn't notice how much time had passed while looking at the game. My phone pinged with a text. I got excited because I knew it was my lil' mama telling me she missed me. Opening the message, it wasn't from Kaymee. It was actually from Poetry.

**Poetry: Dray, I need you to get to Northwestern Memorial. Kaymee was shot. Call ya boy while you're at it because he's not answering me."**

Reading the message, my heart stopped for a second. There was no way I read that correctly. I had to read it again. I hurried to reply because I couldn't believe Kaymee had such a case of bad luck. She was a sweetheart and life just wasn't giving her the opportunity to be great.

**Me: She was shot! How? I'm on my way.**

After texting back immediately, I tossed the remote on the bed and didn't bother turning off the TV. The baseball game was the furthest thing from my mind at that moment. As I put on my shoes, another text came through but I didn't check it. I grabbed my phone and googled the name of the hospital that Poetry mentioned.

I keyed the address into the GPS and snatched my keys up, running for the door. I fumbled with the keys, causing them to slip from my hand as I tried to lock the door. I had to take a few breaths to calm my nerves before retrieving them. Finally locking the door, I hit the key fob to unlock the car door. The way my adrenaline was rushing, moving the car wouldn't be a smart decision. Checking the last text that was sent, I shook my head.

**Poetry: She's in room 412.**

That shit kind of made everything real in my eyes. Not saying Poetry would lie about something like that, but I kind of wished she were. I scrolled up to read the first message again and I saw something that I didn't pay attention to when I read it before. Monty was not with Poetry and he wasn't answering her calls. This nigga was tripping. I hoped he wasn't on bullshit because Poetry didn't seem like the kind of woman that was going to take that shit sitting down.

I called him about ten times back to back like he was *my* nigga and he still didn't answer. He was wasting my time and I needed to get to Kaymee. I started the route on my phone and placed it in my lap. Listening to the directions that were given from the GPS, I finally made it to the hospital without any problems.

All of the parking spots were taken on the street. I had no other choice except to pay for parking in the garage. The money was not an issue. There wasn't any amount that would stop me from going up to check on my girl. Sitting in the car, I tried to reach Monty once more before I stepped out of the car. He still didn't answer. I wasn't about to sit there any longer trying to get him on the line.

Walking into the hospital doors, there was an elderly couple in front of me and I was really getting impatient. I had much respect for older people and I couldn't see myself being disrespectful. I needed to get upstairs or wherever to check on Kaymee. Glancing around the lobby, I took in the huge fish tank that had different kinds of tropical fish in it to keep my mind off snapping on somebody. When I turned back around, the elders were still talking to the person at the counter. My phone rang and I looked down shaking my head.

"Where the hell are you, Monty?" I asked lowly, trying to keep my voice down. I didn't need everyone in my business.

I could hear the wind whipping in the background. That let me know that he was flying on the expressway. "I just got Poetry's text and I saw all the calls from the both of y'all. Where are you and what the hell happened?" he asked.

"I don't know what happened, fam and I'm at Northwestern Memorial where you should be. But you have yet to answer my question. Where the fuck are *you*?"

"Look, don't worry about where the fuck I am! I didn't get the calls or text right away. I'll be there in about ten minutes," he said, hanging up.

Since he said he was ten minutes away, I decided to go outside and wait for him. I wasn't the one that wasn't answering my girl's calls and I didn't appreciate him going in on my ass. Spotting a bench not too far from the door, I took a seat. I took my phone out and scrolled through social media and all I saw up and down my timeline were RIP posts. The shit was sad because I didn't know what shape my girl was in. It didn't stop me from giving my condolences to the families.

"Dray, are you okay?"

I looked up from my phone and Poetry was sitting next to me. She placed her arm on my shoulder and I couldn't begin to say how long she had been sitting there. Her eyes were red as hell and she smelled like weed mixed with a fruity type of scent. I could tell that she was high by just looking at her, but she wore the smell, as well.

"I'm okay. I thought it would be a good idea to wait for Monty. I finally got him on the line and he's on his way. What happened, Poetry?"

"That's what we're trying to find out. All I can tell you is she was shot in the arm. She has to stay here until the swelling goes down so they can set the bone. She has a fracture and she is one lucky girl. There was a guy brought in with her. We couldn't get any information on him because we aren't family.

Deep down, I know it was Jonathan. I called G and told him what's going on and he's on his way."

Hearing what she said brought tears to my eyes because she will be okay. I feared that she was in there fighting for her life, but that wasn't what I had to worry about. Now I had to figure out how to protect her from the things that continuously hurt her. I had to be her protector as well as the one that was willing to love her harder than she had ever been loved before. How I would pull it off was something that I had to figure out.

"Hey, lil' mama. How is Kaymee?"

We both looked up as G made his way over to where we sat. This man's demeanor was so smooth and laid back. Underneath it all, I knew he was a force to be reckoned with. He was here to find out what happened to his family and I didn't think he was leaving until he got the information he was seeking. I didn't blame him because I would be the same way, to be honest.

"Hi, G—" Poetry started speaking to G but stopped mid-sentence as Monty walked from across the street. The fire appeared in her eyes faster than lightening. The transformation of her facial features was sudden and the anger couldn't be missed. Her demeanor changed back to normal at a blink of an eye.

Turning back to G, she started talking again as if she'd never saw him. "Sorry. Hey, G. My mom called me almost a half hour ago saying she woke up. I haven't made it upstairs because I saw Dray sitting here by himself. We can go up now if everyone is ready. You would have to get passes, though," she said, walking away.

We walked up to the counter and received our passes. G asked if there was anyone admitted by the name of Jonathan Dawson and there was. He was in ICU. G was going to have to go up in order to get information on his prognosis. He decided to go up to see Kaymee first to find out what happened. On our way to the elevators, I noticed a gift shop at the end of the hall.

"I'll meet y'all upstairs. I want to go to the gift shop to get my baby something to brighten her day," I said, heading to the shop.

"Hold up, Dray. We'll go with you. We all can bring a ray of sunshine her way," Monty said, walking in Poetry's direction.

He tried to grab her and she moved out of the way and started walking in the direction of the gift shop. She wasn't trying to be in his presence at all. Monty's head hung down as he followed behind her. He lifted his head and ran his hand down his face.

"You good, bro?" I asked him as I caught up with him.

"Yeah, I fucked up when I didn't answer her calls. It wasn't on purpose, but I shouldn't have been doing what I was doing. Don't ask. I don't want to talk about it," he said, glancing in the direction of the gift shop.

She had already disappeared into the shop, so it was safe for him to talk about what was on his mind. We all stopped walking, but Monty didn't say anything. G took the opportunity to spit some logic to him. From the way he stared at Monty, it seemed he knew what was up already. His nostrils flared as he shook his head.

"If you love that girl, Montez, you better leave Mena's ass alone. I don't see anything good coming from you trying to be a playa. The way Mena was acting the day y'all was at the club, I knew there was some history between the two of you. I found out the truth once y'all left. Mena don't lie to me about shit. And she called me and told me how you just left without giving her an explanation tonight. You are playing with fire because Mena loves yo' ass. End that shit before you lose yo' girl," G said, walking off.

I looked at Monty and he stood there as if he was giving me the opportunity to speak my piece. It wasn't my place to say anything to him about what he did. That was his relationship that he was jeopardizing. I would continue to have his back the way I've always done. There wasn't anything I wanted to say. I knew what G said was true because Monty didn't deny anything he said.

"Let's get these gifts so I can see my girl," I said, patting him on the back.

\*\*\*

There were teddy bears and balloons galore in the gift shop. I believe from the four of us, Kaymee had every kind of bear, balloon, card, and snack we put our hands on. She definitely would have a smile on her face the minute we enter her room. In the elevator, I was trying to get the elephant out of the small space when it came to Poetry and my boy. She was ignoring him with a smile on her face.

Exiting the elevator, Poetry led us to Kaymee's room. She peeked her head in and said, "Hey, bestie! You want some company?"

"Yasssss, sis! Bring your butt in here!"

Kaymee's voice sounded like she was forcing herself to be happy, but I didn't care as long as I was able to hear it. Poetry pushed the door open and we all followed behind her. The way Kaymee's eyes lit up when she saw all of us made a smile appear on my face. She had a bandage on her arm and she was hooked up to an IV. The pole had two bags on it, but obviously both were needed.

"Oh my gosh! I didn't expect to see all of you guys! Are those gifts for me?" she said, smiling.

I walked over and gave her the gifts as I kissed her on the lips. She was struggling to sit up, so I helped her by raising the back of the bed and helping her adjust her body. Avoiding her left arm at all cost, I finally got her to a comfortable position. Monty, G, and Poetry gave her the gifts that were bought for her and hugs and kisses were given.

"Y'all just made my day. It's like my birthday all over again," she said, crying. "I thought I was gonna die y'all. Why do things keep happening to me? Wait! Where is my dad? I mean Jonathan?" she said with fear in her eyes.

I looked at G, giving him the go ahead to let her in on what he found out. He stepped forward and grabbed her hand. I saw that he was rubbing his thumb back and forth over her fingers. His eyes were lowered to the floor and it appeared as if he was about to give bad news. The room was silent and everyone was holding their breath.

"He is in ICU, Kaymee. I don't know how he is doing, but I will find out. I wanted to come here to see you first because I need to know what took place. When I'm done with you, I will check on him and come back to let you know his prognosis. Deal?"

Kaymee shook her head up and down. She moved her hand and reached for a tissue on the nightstand. Blowing her nose, she looked at Poetry with the saddest look in her eyes. Poetry took that as her cue, going to the other side of the bed and crawling in beside her.

She looked around the room and her eyes watered again. I felt bad for her because she had to relive what happened to her. This ordeal could either break her or make her stronger. We wouldn't know until we got to that point. All we could do was watch her closely and make sure she was alright. I was wondering why her mother wasn't here. It seemed kind of odd that she wasn't. I hoped she wasn't that cruel not to show up when her daughter had been shot.

"Bae, did anyone call your mother?" I asked.

Her head snapped in my direction and there wasn't a tear in sight. The sadness was quickly replaced with anger. Actually, I saw hate when I mentioned her mother. I didn't know what I had said that what was so wrong, but I shut my mouth from the stare she shot my way.

"That bitch ain't no mother of mine! There's not a mother on this earth that would do what she did to her child!" she screamed. She lowered her voice but the venom remained in her words. "I tolerated her talking to me like I wasn't shit, I even allowed her to put her hands on me for no damn reason, but what I will not accept under any circumstance is the shit she did today. Dot is the person that shot me and my daddy! Why do she hate me so much?" she wailed out.

I didn't know what to say to what she had revealed. Turning my head to look at Monty, the scowl on his face screamed murder. There wasn't going to be any way to stop him from going after her. G's face wasn't any different. I knew from that moment, things were about to get pretty messy in Chicago.

## Chapter 5
## G

When Dray asked Kaymee did she have someone to call her mama, I wasn't expecting the words that came out of her mouth. Monty had already let us in on what had been going on in her life the night before. To hear that Dot had something to do with her and my uncle being laid up in the hospital put me in kill mode. The look in my little cousin's eyes told me that underneath all of that sweetness, she was nothing to play with.

"Come again, Kaymee. I know you didn't say what I thought you said. Please say I heard you wrong," Monty said, walking over to her bed.

"You heard me right, bro. Dot shot my dad and me when we were walking to the truck at Olive Garden on Addison. We had just had a good time catching up and when we walked out the restaurant, she was coming in our direction in the parking lot with a man. She got upset when she saw us together and started trying to fight me. Jonathan told me to go to the truck and I did, but something told me to go back because of the things she was saying. When I got to the back of the truck, I heard a gunshot and I felt something hot on my arm. I fell to the ground and stayed as still as I could. Then I heard another shot and my daddy fell to the ground. Dot and the man took off running and they drove off."

I stood there trying to take all of this in because I wanted to kill this bitch. I didn't want to take the life of her mother but the bitch violated in a major way. You fucked with my family and thought everything was good because you got away. Nah, that's not how shit went down.

"Kaymee, your mama has been doing a lot of shit to you. How about you tell me about that," I said to her.

"I don't want to get all into any of that. The only thing I'm willing to say is that she never loved me. She treated me like I wasn't her daughter and it was all because my daddy didn't want to be with her. He told her to get an abortion, but she insisted on having me. No one made that decision but her. Everybody knows that a baby isn't gonna make a man stay. He told her that he wasn't ready for a child, but she didn't listen. I didn't deserve the treatment she gave me my entire life. The best years of my life came from when I lived with my grandmother. After she died, my life went from sugar to shit from the age of six until now. I hate her for what she has put me through. The doctor says that the police will be here to talk to me. I'm not telling them shit. Do what you have to do, Monty. I'm tired of protecting her when she has never protected me from anything in my life," she said, crying.

"Everything is going to be alright, baby. I promise she will never hurt you again. You are eighteen years old and you will go to college and make something of yourself. You hear me?" Poetry's mom said, walking around the bed. She gathered Kaymee in her arms and let her cry.

Poetry took all of the gifts except one bear off Kaymee's lap and put everything on the dresser. I looked at both Dray and Monty and motioned toward the door. It was time to put a plan in motion. Monty walked over to Poetry and gathered her in his arms. She buried her head in his chest but only briefly. I walked over to tell him that I would meet him outside, but the way Poetry's head reeled back, I knew something was about to go down.

"Now I know why you wasn't answering your phone. You smell just like a bitch. Stay the fuck away from me, Montez," she gritted.

He tried to pull her back into him and she snatched away for the second time that day. Walking into his face, she said, "This is not the time for me to express what I really want to say to your dirty ass. Go back to that bitch because you don't have a spot over here anymore."

She turned around and stood, looking out of the window. Her mother missed the exchange and I was glad about that. I pushed him toward the door so there wouldn't be any more words exchanged between the two of them. Dray gave Kaymee a hug and kissed her lips. He told her he would be back, then he went out the door behind Montez. I stayed back to talk to the ladies for a quick second.

"I want y'all to sit and let Kaymee tell the police that she didn't know who shot her. I don't want them going to look for Dot. I want to find her myself. What she did wasn't cool. She will be taken care of. Is that understood?"

Poetry's mother acted like she wanted to say something but shook her head in agreement. I didn't tell her what would happen to Dot, but her vindictive ass was going to come up missing. She should've thought about what the fuck she'd done before she did it. Bending down to hug Kaymee, I kissed her on the forehead.

"You will be okay, cuz. I promise you that," I said to her and left out of the room.

Monty and Dray was nowhere to be found. I hit them with a text explaining that I was going to check on my uncle and I would meet them outside. Taking the elevator to the Intensive Care Unit, my stomach was knotting up and I suddenly felt like I had to shit. I spent too much damn time in the hospital not too long ago with my wife. I hated not knowing.

When I got to ICU, I was led to Jonathan's room by a nurse and my heart stopped. He was attached to many machines and the tears that clouded my vision cascaded down my face. My nigga was on a fuckin' ventilator and I had to will my feet to move to his bed. This man spent twelve years of his life behind bars and not one day went by that he didn't ask about his daughter. He may not have been there physically, but he took care of that girl from the inside. Then he ran into Dot's bitch ass and ends up laying in a fuckin' hospital bed

I pulled a chair closer to his bed and grabbed his hand. God had to do me one more favor because this was one time I wasn't about to accept a loss. Bowing my head, I dug deep in my soul and talked to the man upstairs from my heart.

"Aye, Father God. I know it seems like I'm always coming to you at a time like this, but it's not even like that. You have gotten me and the ones I love through plenty and I appreciate it all. This man right here hasn't walked on the straight and narrow, but he deserves the opportunity to be the best father he can be to his daughter. Everyone has sinned and you are the one that can forgive them. We've done our share of dirt. I know this Lord. Everyone makes mistakes and I'm asking you to give my uncle another chance. In your name I pray, Amen."

My head was still down and the tears were falling on the floor. I felt a hand on my shoulder and I had to wipe my eyes before looking up. There was a doctor standing beside me looking down at me solemnly. He waited until I was ready to address him. I turned my head and stared at Jonathan before I stood.

"Hey, Doc. What type of injuries are we looking at? He's not looking too good right now but looks can be deceiving, right?" I was pleading with this man without outright doing so. I swear for Dot's sake that he gave me some kind of hope, even though nothing was going to save her from what she had coming to her.

"Let's step outside. I will let you know what's going on with Mr. Dawson," he said, walking out the door.

I glanced at Jonathan once more before I walked out the room. The doctor was waiting for me outside the door. He led me down the hall to a small office and motioned toward a chair for me to sit. He walked around the desk and sat, folding his hands together as he sighed and looked like he was praying. Sitting back in the chair, he raised his hands over his head. This man was getting on my nerves because he acted like he was nervous. In turn, he had me thinking there was no hope for my fam.

"I'm Dr. Armstrong and I am the physician that is overlooking things with Mr. Dawson. When he came in, he had lost a substantial amount of blood. We had to rush him to the operating room immediately. X-rays showed the bullet was lodged in his small intestine. A nasogastric tube was inserted to remove the blood and air that was filling his intestine. He was also hooked up to the respirator machine because his breathing wasn't normal during the surgery. The tube will be removed tomorrow depending on how he breathes on his own. The bullet was removed and we stitched him up. He will have a scar going down the middle of his stomach but other than that, he is expected to make a full recovery. We had to give him a blood transfusion, an IV to prevent dehydration to his organs, as well as antibiotics to prevent infections. Mr. Dawson will be here with us for a couple weeks to make sure he is healing properly without complications."

Hearing everything the doctor said, I was relieved to know that he wasn't on the respirator or I would have a decision to make. I was still scared because these doctors could say one thing and some other shit could happen afterwards. My prayer game is about to be on point. He had to walk out of here.

"Thanks. Dr. Armstrong, is it?" He shook his head yes and I continued talking. "My uncle as of now is doing good, right?" Again, he shook his head confirming the question I asked. I couldn't do anything except take his word that Jonathan was going to pull through. "I am Grant Davenport. Mr. Dawson is my uncle. I will be handling all of his doctor bills, so send everything to me," I said, reaching for a pad and a pen. Writing my information down, I ripped it off and handed it to him. "I will be back later to give you a list of people that can visit him. Until then, no one other than myself or Demarius Jones is allowed in his room."

"Understood. Mr. Dawson is in good hands. He will be all right," he said, standing up.

"I hope so," I said, walking out after thanking him and shaking his hand.

# Meesha

## Chapter 6
### Mena

"Girl, I still can't believe Montez hasn't hit my line. Usually when he comes home, I'd know as soon as he touched down. Not this time. I had to see this nigga by accident. On top of that, he had that lil' young bitch with him. It's not like he didn't know I worked at the damn club. I knew G didn't schedule me for that damn party purposely, but it's alright. I will have him over here eating out my ass today."

I was on the phone talking to my girl Cheri as I laid across my bed. Montez was my focal point for the past week and it was driving me crazy. I could still smell the Gucci cologne that he wore that day. When he walked into the club, I didn't see anything but him. Not thinking, I ran straight to him and wrapped my arms around his neck. I melted into his body when he squeezed me tight. It had been a couple months since he snuck in without his little girlfriend knowing and I was glad to see him.

His girl cleared her throat, messing up our union. The way he pulled away from me, one would have thought he was caught stealing. He brought her forward and introduced us. I didn't care who she was to be honest. It was good to finally put a face to the person the nigga was always reminding me he was with. When he was with me, it was *his girl who*? He was never thinking about her ass until she called. That was when his ass would always say, "It's my girl. Don't say shit," before he answered the phone. I blame myself for letting that shit go on for so long.

Being a twenty-three-year-old bartender that worked at the hottest club in Chicago, I shouldn't have been running up behind a nigga that didn't want me as his woman. I set myself up when I was cool being the side chick to his ass. That nigga couldn't even take her young ass to the club, so I knew she wasn't satisfying him the way I did. He wouldn't be going back to Atlanta without saying he wanted to be with me. Leaving me alone was not an option.

"Mena! Did you hear what I said? I hate when you do that! Get ya mind right. I've been talking to myself for the past five minutes!" Cheri screamed in my ear.

"I'm sorry. My mind drifted. I didn't hear you. What did you say?"

"I said, fuck that nigga to be frank. You are forever sniffing behind his ass and he doesn't want anything but one thing. He comes through, fuck, and get ghost. Is that all you're worth? There are so many niggas that want to get to know you, but you're waiting on a nigga that's already in a relationship. You are beautiful, Mena. Five foot six, one hundred forty-five pounds with a big dumb ass. You are always slaying around this bitch. You make your own money and have been taking care of yourself for years. You don't need him. The little things he does for you ain't shit. Leave his ass alone before shit goes left," Cheri practically begged me

Everything Cheri said was true, but I couldn't do anything to stop what my heart wanted. It just so happened to be screaming for Montez. He would be back in between my legs before the day was over. I had to work tonight and I knew that I needed to make this happen before the night ended. I wasn't leaving him alone, so she could stop with the prep talk. I wasn't trying to hear none of that.

"I hear what you are saying Cheri, but I don't want them other niggas! I've invested two years of my life with Montez. I'm not giving up. We were meant to be together."

"You sound stupid as fuck, Mena. I wouldn't be a real friend if I didn't tell you the real. Stop being stupid for his ass. You have been playing the back position too long, waiting for his ass to choose you. He has made his choice. He ain't leaving his girl, period. The only thing y'all were meant to be was fuck buddies. If you are cool with that, then who am I to tell you different?" she said, sighing loudly.

Knowing she was pissed off, I changed the subject. I didn't want to have this ongoing argument with her. "Are you coming to the club tonight? There's gonna be a full house. Niggas are gon' be all through that bitch."

"I hope one of them grab your attention. You need a nigga to take your mind off Montez. You deserve to be happy, Mena. The man upstairs didn't stop making men when they made him. I don't know how your feelings got involved anyway. Then again, I remember that one picture you showed me of his dick and that muthafucka was mouthwatering," she said, laughing.

"Not gonna happen, sis and for the record, I am happy. Being happy comes from within. A nigga is an added addition, thank you very much. I didn't show you that picture for you to speak on his pipe either. Forget you ever saw that shit. Now, I have things to do. I will see you later at the club. I love ya, boo and please, let me deal with my situationship with Montez," I said, rolling onto my back.

"I hear you, Diva. Just be careful. I would hate to have to put hands on a muthafucka. I'll talk to you later and I love you too, stupid ass," she said, hanging up.

She knew to hang the fuck up before I went in on her ass. Cheri knew that I didn't play. She got a pass and that was because she was my bitch. I blamed myself for the way she spoke her mind, I was always telling her everything when I was in my feelings. Sometimes I needed to keep shit to myself, it was hard to accomplish though. I needed to talk about what I was going through and she was my right hand, there was no one else I would ever tell my business to.

Resting my eyes, a vision of Montez flashed behind my lids. My kitty jumped a couple times and I grabbed it as a groan escaped my lips. I removed my boy shorts before opening my legs wide. I played with kitty until she was nice and wet, then I snapped a picture with a smile on my face. I sent the picture to him with the caption, "Cum lick her clean, Zaddy". He texted back, letting me know he was on his way. I almost broke my neck running to the bathroom to shower.

I washed quickly and jumped out. Not bothering to put on any clothes, I rubbed Michael Kors Sexy Ruby lotion all over my body. When I finished oiling my feet, I heard a car pull into my driveway. Walking briskly to the door, I opened it and didn't have a stitch of clothing on. Montez looked around trying to see if anyone was out I guess, but his movement never ceased. I licked my lips because he was looking good enough to eat and I was ready to devour his ass.

He grabbed me around the waist and pushed me into the house. I heard the door slam shut and the lock clicking in place. He bent down and stuck his tongue in my mouth. The taste of cherry was in his mouth and it was delicious. I reached for his buckle and I couldn't get it open to save my life. He had to do it himself while he had his finger all up my ass.

The way he worked my body over for the next hour had me spent. I was looking forward to us lying in bed cuddling for the night but that didn't happen. He fell on top of his clothes and rolled over to retrieve his phone from his shorts. He looked at it long enough to read a text then jumped up racing to the bathroom. When he came out, he didn't even acknowledge me. I wasn't about to let him leave without giving me an explanation.

I grabbed his arm before he could get out of the door. "It's like that? You just gon' hit and leave?" I asked looking in his eyes.

He told me that he couldn't explain things and he would call me later, then he was out the door and in his car. I felt like he played me and I was tired of his shit. I slammed the door, went to my room, and ran me a hot bath. I wasn't about to let him worry me with his bullshit. "The way he just worked every inch of my body, he couldn't be loving that bitch too much," I said to myself as I added bubbles to the water and stepped into the tub.

56

The bath relaxed my mind and my body, I ended up falling asleep and had less than an hour to get ready and get to the club. My skin was wrinkled like a prune and the water was iced cold. I pulled the stopper out and turned the water on to shower. I hurried and washed as fast as I could and hopped out. Snatching my towel off the rack, I dried off as I ran to the closet in my bedroom. I grabbed one of my black GSpot tees and a pair of black jeans with holes in them. I didn't bother putting on any panties as I retrieved a black bra from the dresser. After putting it on, I pulled on my pants and shirt and sprayed on a little Sexy Ruby perfume. Running a comb through my long weave and applying a little gloss on my lips, I threw my phone in my purse and headed for the door. My keys were on the kitchen counter and I scooped them up and kept going.

I made it to the club with twenty minutes to spare before the doors were scheduled to open. The other two bartenders were already getting things set up. Lisa rolled her eyes when she saw me because she thought she hit a lick. See, I worked the main bar by myself and the money poured in all night. She was probably hoping and praying I didn't show. Oh, how wrong she was.

"It's about time you showed up *after* I've set your shit up," she sassed with her hand on her hip.

"We will not do this tonight, Lisa. I'm quite sure you took it upon yourself to do what you did only because you didn't think I was coming. Thanks anyway, boo but get yo' mad ass away from me," I said, turning my back on her

"I guess I have to get me a Goon to fuck in order to get special treatment," she said with a smirk on her face.

"This is my muthafuckin' spot and it doesn't matter who's fuckin' and suckin'. There is no special treatment. It's either you work your ass off to get this money, or you go home broke. This is not the hoe spot. It's the GSpot. Leave that shit outside."

When the deep baritone filled my ears, I turned and stared at Lisa to see what she had to say. She stood at the end of the bar looking like a damn fool. G didn't play that petty shit, but she seemed to always get caught talking a lot of it.

"Well, why do Mena always get to work the main bar? Explain that shit, G."

He stared at her and his jawline was flexing strong. "I don't have to explain shit to you, Lisa but I will. Mena has been working with me three years. You, on the other hand, have been working here three months. When you stop costing me money by breaking shit and barely working, then holla at me. Until then, yo' ass will be in that lil' ass corner where I assigned you. If you don't like it, quit. I won't miss you because you do more partying than working. That shit ends tonight, or you will be paying your way in to shake your ass. I don't want to hear anything else about how I run my establishment. Now go where you're supposed to be," he said, never taking his eyes off of her.

I smirked at her ass and she stormed off. G was still standing in the same spot and I knew he was about to go in on me next. Making eye contact, I waited for him to say what he had to say and I had a feeling it was about Montez.

"Mena, I want you to stay the fuck away from Monty. You knew from the gate that he had a girl. I know how you roll and I don't need that bullshit around my establishment, legal or illegal. I already talked to that nigga. Now, I'm speaking to you. End that shit," he said, walking away without giving me a chance to speak.

If he thought what Montez and me had was going to stop because he said so, he was out of his damn mind. I wasn't going to be able to shut my love off for that nigga like a water faucet. It wasn't going to be that easy. Plus, I didn't want to stop fucking with him. My body only responded to the way he caressed it. I regretted bringing up Montez in the conversation that I had with G after Montez left my house. Now he was going to be on me every time something went wrong with us.

Since my bar was fully stocked, I took the opportunity to give Montez a call since I hadn't heard from him since he left

58

earlier. Not to mention, G had put him back on my mind with his speech. His phone rang a couple times and I knew I was sent to voicemail with a touch of the decline button. It only made me hit the call button again and each time, I got the same results. He knew I didn't like when he ignored me for that bitch. I called a couple more times before I finally left a message.

"Montez, you know damn well I don't like to be ignored. The least you can do is pick up the damn phone and tell me you can't talk. I didn't see your ass ignoring me when you had your tongue deep in my muthafuckin' pussy! Don't fuck with me and I won't fuck with what you got going on with that bitch! Call me back!" I barked into the phone.

When he did call back, he was going to have a nasty ass attitude, but I didn't give a fuck. What he wasn't about to do was treat me like I didn't mean anything to him. I would no longer be available only when he wanted to deal with me. That shit was dead. I didn't have time for the bullshit. "He'd better be ready to deal with me whenever the fuck I called his ass," I said to myself as the doors to the club opened for business.

# Meesha

## Chapter 7
### Montez

Dray and I left out of Kaymee's room and went outside so I could smoke and get my mind right. The way Poetry looked at me was embedded in my mind. She had been upset with me on plenty occasions, but I'd never seen that particular glare before. The words that spewed from her mouth shocked the shit out of me because I didn't notice that I had Mena's scent on me. I was careful about showering before I left, but up until a few minutes ago, I didn't think about her hugging me when I stepped inside her crib.

I was mad at myself because after two years, I had never been caught fucking around on her. I loved Poetry with all my heart, but there was something about Mena that I couldn't shake. Her pussy was like a drug that I was addicted to. There were times that I came home and Poe never knew I was in the city. I would spend my entire stay with Mena.

The shit was wrong and I knew it, but why stop fucking with her if I was getting away with the shit? I had an advantage because Poe was younger and she had a curfew. It was easy for me to spend the day with her then spend the night with Mena. Basically, I had my cake and I ate the shit out of it.

"You want to talk about what's on yo' mind, fam?" Dray asked, cutting into my thoughts.

"Poetry smelled Mena's perfume on me and she told me to go back to the bitch. She all but said she was done fuckin' with me. I'm slippin', my nigga. I got rid of all the bitches back in Atlanta because I knew my baby was coming down to Spelman. My stupid ass come home and get caught the fuck up at a crucial time at that. I don't know how the fuck I'm gon' make this shit right."

I pulled a blunt from my pocket and flamed it up as I started walking down the street. As we walked, both of us received a text at the same time. I didn't give a fuck about checking mine, but Dray checked his. All I wanted to do was smoke and try to clear my head.

"That was G saying that he is on his way down," Dray said.

Not giving a fuck, I continued walking and puffing. I started getting mad all over again because I started thinking about what Dot did to Kaymee. She did many things to that girl, but this time she fucked up royally. I had wanted to beat the fuck out of her and Kaymee stopped me every time. This was the last straw because when the one person that was saving your ass, gives the go ahead, there was no rules to what I could do.

"Montez!"

I turned around after hearing my name being called. I saw G standing by the hospital entrance and headed back. As bad as I wanted to go into the hospital to talk to Poetry, I knew it would be a bad idea. Letting her cool off was a better option at the moment. We weren't set to leave for school for three weeks. That was plenty of time to get shit back on track before we headed down south.

Standing in front of G, he explained Jonathan's condition to us and I felt bad because he had to go through that shit. Hearing that he was expected to make a full recovery was a big relief. I was glad I wouldn't have to break any bad news to Mee. The information that G revealed gave me the excuse to go back to Mee's room. Then I could talk to my girl, too.

"A'ight, I'm going in to give Mee the good news. Before I go back up, what's the plan for Dot's hoe ass?" I asked G, hitting the last of the blunt.

"Yo' ass ain't slick, nigga. I already told Kaymee about Jonathan. There's no reason for you to go back in there tonight. Poetry will be staying with her and the doctor came back in to check on her arm. The swelling is going down very well and they may be able to set her bone in the morning. Give ya girl time to calm down."

"I need to make this shit right though, G. I fucked up," I said.

"That you did, lil' homie. Today is not gon' make every-thing better. Take my word on that. You are gon' have to let her decide on her own what she wants to do. Forcing her or demanding shit will only worsen the situation. What you need to do is put a stop to the shit you got going on with Mena. Eve-rything is all good with the other woman until you want to end things. Be ready for whatever drama comes your way because you brought this shit on yourself."

I couldn't even argue with what he was saying because he was only speaking the truth. Mena wasn't going to cause any problems because she knew I had a girl from day one. We even had a conversation a while back about if we had to end things. She said it wouldn't be a problem if I didn't want to see her anymore. That was something I wasn't worried about. My cell-phone continued to vibrate and I took it off my hip. I had sev-eral calls from Mena and a voicemail. I placed it back on my hip without listening to it.

"As far as Dot goes, we will meet up at GSpot tonight at eleven. I will let it be known what will go down with that. Don't be late and take yo' ass home until it's time to hit the club. Another thing, stay the fuck away from Mena!" he said, pointing in my face.

"I hear ya, fam. I'm going home to clear my mind for a couple of hours. I'm sleepy anyway." I took my keys from my pocket as we walked to the parking garage.

The three of us jumped in our cars and hit the road. G got on the expressway going south and Dray and I got on head-ing north. The entire ride to the crib, my phone was blowing up and every time it was Mena. I was not in the mood to talk to her. This shit wasn't her fault because she didn't force a muthafucka to cheat.

Pulling up in the driveway I cut off the engine and sat in the car for a minute. I thought about Poetry not fucking with me after this and a nigga low key wanted to cry. I shook that thought from my head because we had been together too long to break up after one mistake. This was not the end for us, it couldn't be.

Dray knocked on my window and I glanced over at him. He didn't wait for me to get out. He went inside and closed the door. Grabbing the loud out the armrest with two packs of swishers, I made my way inside. A smile spread across my face when I looked in the corner of the living room. All the presents that Mee didn't open for her birthday were still sitting waiting to be opened. I was going to take some of them to the hospital tomorrow to brighten her day again.

I walked to the money case and decided to see how much she had in it. Placing it on the coffee table, I took out my keys and unlocked it. I separated the bills by denominations and started counting. When I finished, she had a total of five racks and that didn't include the money that I had in the room from her dress. I picked up the case, turned the light out, and headed to my room. I went to my safe and keyed in the code. I had put Mee's money in a manila envelope. I emptied it on the bed and counted the bills. Altogether she had damn near ten racks. I went back to the safe and put the difference in the case making it an even ten.

Locking the case, I sat it in my closet and took off my clothes. I laid down and picked up my phone. Pressing the button for the voicemail, I listened to the bullshit that Mena had to say. I shook my head and ran my hand down my face. *"What the fuck did I get myself into?"* I thought to myself as I reached over and grabbed the loud along with the swishers. I needed to roll a fat one for the bullshit I was enduring.

Mena was out of her fuckin' mind if she thought her threats meant anything to me. She needed to continue to play her position before she got her muthafuckin' feelings hurt. This wasn't a problem she wanted to create. I didn't lie to her about anything. The woman that I lied to was Poetry and she was the only one that I owed an explanation to. I didn't owe Mena shit.

I dialed Poetry's number listening to the phone ring. She let her phone ring all the way out until the voicemail picked up. I pressed the end button and dialed again. When the phone started to ring, it was immediately sent to voicemail. That was something I wasn't used to and it didn't sit well with me. I dial her number again and she answered. My heart started beating fast because I knew she wouldn't keep ignoring me.

"Montez, I want you to stop calling my phone. I don't have shit to say to you right now. If you didn't want to be with me, that's all your ass had to say. I'm the type of bitch that don't try to keep a nigga that don't wanna be kept. You are free to keep doing what you were doing earlier with whomever you were out entertaining. When you are single, you get to do what the fuck you want to do. Keep doing you, my nigga. Now get the fuck off my phone!"

"Poetry, baby, it wasn't even like that. I didn't do anything wrong. I ran into someone that I knew back when and she gave me a hug. That's all it was, baby, I swear."

When I didn't hear her say anything, I looked at the screen and the backlight wasn't even on. She hung up after she said what she had to say. She wasn't trying to hear me. I knew that I had some serious ass kissing to do before she would forgive me.

I pressed the button to bring my phone back to life and looked at the time. It was nine-thirty and I had to be at the club at eleven. There was no way I was going to be able to take a nap and get up on time. I decided to look through the pictures of me and Poetry that I had in my phone until I got up to take a shower. I broke the weed down and rolled up, flaming up as I got lost in my thoughts.

*** 

Tired was an understatement of how I was feeling. I should've taken my ass to sleep for an hour at least because I didn't feel like doing shit. I couldn't call G up and tell him I couldn't make it because he wouldn't go for that shit. My ass needed to be front and center when he ran down the plan for

Dot. I was ready to fight for my sis on this one just like any other time.

Mena had been calling and texting my phone nonstop. Telling her that we couldn't continue the way we had been was going to be hard. I was sending prayers up that she took it for what it was. The shit that we were doing was fun while it lasted but it had to end. I was sloppy and I got called out on my shit. Facing Poetry about my infidelity was what I was worried about at that point. Anything else was irrelevant.

My phone continued to ring as I rumbled through my clothes trying to find something to wear. Like clockwork, a text came through when I didn't answer. The way my phone was going off, I knew I had plenty of missed calls and just as many text messages from Mena. I dreaded the conversation that we needed to have about us.

I received a complimentary text as I snatch a pair of black Balmain jeans from the hanger. It wasn't anyone but Mena and I knew it without checking. She was about to be on bullshit and I wasn't in the mood for the childish shit. Choosing an olive-green polo shirt to wear, I grabbed the shoebox that held my Gucci sneakers off the floor.

Dressing quickly, I hurried to the bathroom, brushed my teeth, and washed my face. I applied a little bit of Olive oil crème moisturizer to my hair and brushed it. My waves had to be on point. I washed and dried my hands and went back to my bedroom. Pulling my platinum and diamond chain over my head, I secured the matching bracelet on my wrist.

Glancing in the mirror, my eyes fell upon the picture of Poetry and me from years ago. The smile that graced her lips didn't disappear earlier today. I felt like shit for what I had been doing to her. She was never supposed to find out. Coming home to change was not on my mind when I read the text about Kaymee. Two years of getting away with shit and I got caught off a technicality.

"I'm glad you're not in too much pain. I'll be there first thing in the morning to see you baby," Dray said as he came down the hall. When he made it to my doorway, he was listening to the person on the phone. "Fam, Kaymee says hello and you need to fix that," he said, while staring at me.

"What's up, sis and ya girl got that in the palm of her hand."

I wasn't about to discuss that with Mee because she wasn't the one with the problem. I tried to address the situation, but Poetry told me not to call her anymore. It wasn't something that I planned to continue doing, but for tonight, that's how it would be. Dray was about to repeat something else that Mee said, but I wasn't about to keep responding to the shit.

"Let's go. We got moves to make," I said, turning off the light and walking out the door.

He was still talking to Mee as I left out and headed to my car. Climbing into the driver seat, I cranked up my ride and "Confessions" by Usher blared through the speakers. I hit another button to change the station and "Bust Your Windows" by Jazmine Sullivan started playing. I looked up at the roof of my car and yelled, "Damn, man! I get it! I fucked up! Tell me something I don't know."

Dray ended the call with Mee and climbed into the passenger seat. After he closed the door, I threw the car in reverse and peeled out of the driveway, heading to the club. I didn't give a fuck if Dray was completely inside that muthafucka or not. The song continued to play and I turned the radio off completely. Poetry wasn't crazy enough to fuck with my car. I wasn't worried about that. This whole dilemma was fucking with my mental, though.

As I pulled into a spot at the club, my phone started ringing. I looked down and it was Mena. Dray got out of my ride and went into the club. The parking lot was filled to capacity and the line was wrapped around the building. How the fuck did she have the time to constantly blow my shit up? It was ten minutes to eleven and I found myself going through the messages.

**Mena: I know you see all my calls. It will be wise for you to call me back.**

**Mena: Montez! I know muthafuckin' well you are not ignoring me for that bitch! Call me back.**

**Mena: The last thing you want to do is piss me off!**

**Mena: I have played second fiddle to this lil' bitch for two years. This shit stops now! You belong to me!**

My blood was boiling after I read the last message. I couldn't believe she switched up on a nigga like that. She was acting as if she didn't know that I had a woman. There wasn't one time I gave her an indication that I was going to ever leave Poe to be with her. Now she wanted to stake claim like I had been feeding her false hope. I was straight up with her from the start and now she wanted to act clueless. The only thing I knew was she'd better stay in her muthafuckin' lane before I laid hands on her.

Looking at the dash, I noticed the time was eleven o'clock. Fucking around with those damn messages, the time flew past. I jumped out of the car and hit the button on the key fob to lock my doors. I walked up to the door and dapped up Bo at the door.

"What up, Monty? Gon' in. You the last one to arrive. Everyone else is upstairs in the office," he said, attending to the next person in line.

I walked through the crowd and threw a quick glance toward the main bar. Mena was busy handling drink orders, but the frown on her face was on display for everyone to see. That was my cue to get to the steps. I climbed them two at a time so I wouldn't be seen. I knocked on the door and it opened swiftly.

"Damn, Similac. You don't know how to get to this muthafucka on time? You slippin'," Scony said, moving aside so I could enter.

"I'm not in the mood for yo' shit, Scony," I said, bumping past him.

"When you are on my muthafuckin' time, you don't come in this bitch with ya mood swings. Yo' mood should always be

68

set to Goon when yo' ass is coming to conduct business. That other shit should've been left at the doe, nigga."

Scony was standing nose to nose with me, but I wasn't about to back down from his ass. My arms came up and I pushed him hard in his chest. He stumbled a bit and came back at me full force. Before he could hit me, G jumped in the middle and blocked his fist with the palm of his hand. He looked back and forth between the two of us with the meanest scowl on his face.

"Save that shit for the streets. This is not what the fuck we are here for. We are a muthafuckin' unit. We go hard at other niggas, not our own! Both of y'all better buck the fuck down!"

I glared at Scony then I turned to find a place to sit. I felt the back of my neck being grabbed and I snatched away turning around fast. G stood with his head cocked to the side and his jaws clenched. He looked like a pitbull ready to attack. My shoulders relaxed once I saw it was him.

"Monty, I don't know what the fuck is going on, but we don't leave shit like this unresolved. Both of you muthafuckas better squash this shit and it better get squashed now! As Scony said before, whatever is going on in your life, leave that shit outside. Make that shit happen so I can conduct business in this bitch."

I walked over to Scony and held my hand out until he grabbed it to shake up. He pulled me in for a brotherly hug. "My bad, fam. I'm going through some shit right now. I shouldn't have taken that shit out on you. I was late and that was on me."

"Pull that shit again and we gon' be two fighting muthafuckas around here, Similac," he said, letting me go. I went back to the chair I was sitting in and focused on G.

"A'ight, now that we got that bullshit out the way, I wanted to let y'all in on how we are gon' approach this situation with Dot. The shit she did to my fam is not one that will be taken lightly. The bitch got an open invitation to hell. My uncle is laid up along with my cousin. When I saw him in that hospital bed, my emotions were all over the place. He's gonna pull through. We just have to be patient and wait. They will take the tube out tomorrow to see if he will breath on his own, so it's not as bad as it looked. I thought it over and I think he should have a say in what happens to Dot," G said, looking in my direction.

I was listening to everything with murder on my mind. All the things that she had put Mee through started clouding my mind. I was ready to choke the snot out of her ass. "Why wait? Let's just kill her ass," I shot back at him.

"Nah, that's too easy and I believe Jonathan's gonna agree once I talk to him. We will allow her to live her life worry free, for now. Right about now, she's not even at the crib. She is somewhere hiding out because she knows she's wrong as two left shoes. Once Jonathan is able to move around, we will pounce. Yes, I'm speaking that shit into existence. If things change, then we will kill the bitch."

"Well, I bet not see her in the streets. I can't promise to act accordingly," I said to G and I was dead serious.

"That's exactly what you will do. This may not get re-solved until after y'all leave to go back down south. Don't worry. I will keep you in the loop. Until then, don't touch a hair on that hoe's body. She will destroy herself, believe that shit. How about y'all go down and have a good time down-stairs. Monty, remember what I told you."

I looked at G and smirked. He was really trying to block. I wasn't thinking about that damn girl. I was already in the dog-house. "Nah, Boss. I'm about to head home. Ain't nothing here for me. I'm in enough trouble as is," I said, laughing as I stood up from the chair.

"A'ight, because I think ya girl can whoop yo' ass to be real with you," he said, while chuckling.

"Get the fuck outta here with that bullshit, nigga! I'm a lover not a fighter. Now I'd beat the shit out of Dot's ass with-out thinking it over," I said, walking out of the door laughing.

"Let's roll Dray before I think too hard about paying Dot a visit."

"Stay the fuck away from that bitch, Montez!" G yelled out.

I bounced down the stairs while taking in the crowd that was in the club. There were plenty of bad bitches that were scantily dressed and turning the fuck up that night. Had a nigga tempted to stay a little longer and have a drink. I paused and took everything in and decided to do just that.

"Yo, fam. You want to chill for a while? I'm not ready to go home to an empty house right now."

"I'm down for whatever. I can use a beer or two so I won't think about Kaymee too much. As a matter of fact, let's go outside first so I can call to make sure she's good."

Nodding my head, I led the way out the door. I headed to my ride and got in to get the blunt I had in the armrest. This nigga was cakin' with sis and he had a big ass smile on his face. I loved that Mee had somebody that was willing to ride for her. They could go far if Dray didn't fuck up. He had hoes just as I did back in Atlanta and he was going to have a little bit of drama when he returned with Mee on his arm. It's on him to nip that shit in the bud on sight.

"A'ight, I'm good now. Let's go back in and have fun for a couple hours. It's almost one, so we can bounce at three. That would give you enough time to clear yo' muthafuckin' head. We're going to the back because I saw ole girl eyeing you as we were leaving. I'm with G on that one. Baby girl seems like trouble. Cut that shit short with her man."

"Make sure you take heed to your own advice before we get back to the south, nigga. I don't need ya hoes fuckin' with my sis."

"Don't worry about that. I have all of that under control," he said, waiting for me to get out.

Snubbing out the blunt, I put it in the door of my ride and we made our way to the entrance. As I reached for the door, it opened and out walked Mena. My hand fell to my side with a heavy thud. I didn't have the energy for her shit. She only came out to see if I was still in the lot. Putting on a show with her ass was something I wasn't about to do.

"Montez, I know you saw my calls and text messages! Why didn't you answer them?" She put her hand on her hip and held her head to the side like that meant something to me

"Mena, leave this shit alone, okay? I didn't respond because I didn't feel a need to."

"Oh, so fuckin' me and dippin' out is the new shit you on, since when?" she asked, raising her voice. She looked at Dray and rolled her eyes. "Would you give us some privacy? He don't need a bodyguard."

"Check yo'self, Mena! He hasn't done nothing to warrant you talking sideways to him. He would have every right to slap you in the mouth if he wanted to and I wouldn't have a muth-fuckin' thing to say about it. That's neither here nor there. He don't need to leave because we're going back inside," I said, reaching for the door.

She slapped my arm down with force to prevent me from opening the door. I almost forgot she was a female when I drew my fist back, but I put it down, turned, and headed to my whip. Staying at the club was not even an option anymore. If I stayed, I would end up hurting her ass. I made it to my car and opened the door. Mena was right behind me trying to jump in around my body.

"What is your problem, Mena? Shouldn't you be inside working?" I yelled at her as I pushed her back.

"All I want to do is talk to you, but you are trying to avoid me. I'm not understanding why. Is it because of that bitch that you're with? I bet she don't make you feel like I do, Montez. She can't be taking care of her muthafuckin' business if you are between my legs every chance you get. The satisfaction is guaranteed over here. Leave that bitch alone and bring yo' ass home, Montez."

She started rubbing up and down my chest seductively, then she grabbed my dick and massaged it through my pants.

When she tried to kiss me on the side of my neck, I slapped her hand down, moved to the side, and closed my door. My joint was telling me to bend her ass over the back of my ride and give her what she wanted, but the way my relationship was set up, it wasn't a wise choice.

"This thing that we have going on has to stop tonight. I can't see you like that no more. I love my girl and I will do what needs to be done to stay in her good graces. It was good while it lasted, but this is the end of the line. I'm sorry that it has to be this way, but my heart is with Poetry, not you," I said, staring in her eyes.

"Two years of fucking me and you don't love me? You can keep repeating it over and over that you don't have feelings for me and you still wouldn't believe the bullshit you just said. That young bitch don't make you happy. I don't know what type of hold she has on you, but she may as well get ready to let you go. You belong to me and the sooner you realize that shit, the better off you will be. There's no way you can fuck me the way you do and just walk away."

"Hold the fuck up. You can stop disrespecting my woman by calling her all these bitches. Your problem is not with her. She don't even know your ass. Direct that shit my way. I'm the one that was putting this long stroke on ya ass. That's the reason you mad, it's not because I'm staying with her. This dick gon' be out ya muthfuckin' life and now you wanna act crazy. To answer your question, no I don't love you. Do I care about you? Yes, I do. That's as far as it goes. Now shawty, you better get your shit together and just walk away because this between us is over," I said, swinging my finger back and forth between the two of us.

I looked around the parking lot and that nigga Dray wasn't out there anymore. Whenever he came back, I was going to fuck him up! I looked back down at Mena and the tears were streaming down her face. I felt bad for what was happening but my decision was final.

"You're seriously gonna walk away from me like this? Montez don't make me beg you to stay with me. I love you so much and I love what we have."

"I have to walk away. You knew that I had a woman from the beginning. You were the one that said you didn't give a fuck about my girl because that was my problem. Now you want to stand here and play the victim. As far as you loving me, you don't love me, Mena. There's plenty of lust floating between us. We got a sexual connection that I won't deny, but that's about all we have. You can save your breath with the begging shit too because it won't make me back out of what I'm doing. This is it. There's no way around it."

She stood there for a minute with her face balled up and her hands clinched into fists. I braced myself because I knew she was going to start swinging any minute. The door to the club opened and out walked G. I saw him heading in our direction but she didn't. I didn't bother to tell her either.

"Mena!" G yelled when he was a few steps away from my car. "What the fuck are you doing out here? I pay you to take care of the busiest bar in my establishment and you're out here on some other shit! Get inside before I send you home permanently!" he shouted across the lot.

It was as if she didn't hear anything he said to her, she didn't budge. Instead, she swung and slapped the shit out of me. G grabbed her by the back of her neck and pushed her toward the club. She turned back around with a sinister grin on her face. All I could do was shake my head at her.

"You can say that you are done with me, but I know better, Montez. I'll see you soon, baby," she said, walking into the club after blowing a kiss at me

Dray whistled and ran his hand across his head. "Damn, brah. She is about to be trouble."

"Shut the fuck up! Don't you think I know this shit already? I didn't know she felt that way about me. We've never exchanged those words, ever. I love one woman and that's Poetry!" I shouted in frustration.

"I told yo' ass to stay the fuck away from her! I also told you that she loved yo' ass, too. Didn't any woman in your family ever tell yo' ass not to give these hoes all the dick? If it's not yo' bitch, you ration that shit out in small portions. I bet you gave her ass the royal treatment like she was yo main chick, but look where that shit got you. You young muthafuckas gon' learn to listen some damn time. Get ready for the dumb shit to unfold because it's coming. Go home, Montez. It wouldn't be wise to go back inside. I'll get up with you later when I'm on my way to the hospital."

He walked off and I got in my car and cranked it up. Staring straight ahead until Dray got in, I pressed on the gas and sped out of the lot as soon as his door closed. All I wanted to do was get to the crib so I could smoke and drink until I passed out.

Meesha

Love Shouldn't Hurt 2

## Chapter 8
### Poetry

Waking up on the couch bed after spending the night with my best friend, I went to the bathroom and brushed my teeth. I walked back to the couch bed and stared out the window. My mind wandered to the events of the night before, but the only scene that played back was the one between Montez and me. All of my senses were intact, so I knew I smelled a bitch on that nigga's shirt without a doubt. When he hugged me, I almost slapped the hell out of him, but I had to keep my cool because I didn't want to act a fool. There was a time and place for everything. I was in the hospital to make sure my best friend was good, nothing else.

I had been trying to keep my mind away from the fact that he was with a bitch after he left me hot and horny to conduct business. My woman's intuition kicked in, but he put that shit on the radar with his actions. I wasn't about to be one of them bitches that forgave a nigga for going out and getting that shit called new pussy. He would never think it's okay to have me out in these streets looking stupid. I hope the bitch was worth losing me for though.

The first person that came to mind was the female at the club. They were too damn cozy that day for my liking. It's been almost a week since I witnessed that encounter. A blind man could see that there was something going on with them. If nothing was going on now, something has happened in the past. Regardless of when, I knew whatever the case, they were together within the last four years. She wasn't someone that was from the neighborhood and she damn sure didn't go to high school with us.

There was a knock on the door, and then it opened. I turned my head and Dr. Reid walked in with a nurse behind him. Kaymee was still sleeping and I didn't blame her. It was six in the morning. If I didn't have bullshit on my mind, I'd still be sleeping, too. I watched while he took the bandage off her arm to

77

examine her wound. Kaymee opened her eyes and glared at him.

"Good morning, Kaymee. How are you feeling this morning?" Dr. Reid asked.

"My arm hurts every time I move. Can I please have something for the pain?"

The pain on her face was evident and it hurt me because there was nothing I could do to take it away. Dr. Reid raised her arm off the bed and she screamed out, "Aaaarghhh!" Tears started flowing down her cheeks and her head fell onto the pillow.

"I'm sorry, Kaymee. We will be going into the operating room to set your arm in about thirty minutes. Then you can heal and get on with your life. How does that sound?" Dr. Reid said with a smile.

"I'm ready when you are," she said, lowly.

I walked over with a tissue and wiped her tears away. Wanting to cry myself, I held her hand to let her know I would forever be there for her. We'd been through so much together and it wouldn't stop that day.

"There will be an anesthesiologist coming to prep you shortly, then it will be game time. I will make sure you are as good as new, Kaymee. Is there a specific color cast that you would like to wear for the next couple of months?"

"Olive green would be a perfect color for her. It's her favorite and it would go with her chucks," I said, laughing.

"Yeah, what she said," Kaymee said, chuckling.

"You got it, pretty lady. I'll be back to fetch you in a little while. Be patient because it's almost healing time," he said, patting her on the top of her head.

Once he was gone I looked down at Kaymee and smiled. I was glad she was about to get her arm set because I wanted to get out of this hospital. It was time for me to pay Dot a visit so I could ask her what the fuck her problem was. Before I could say what was on my mind, the door opened and two police officers walked in. I forgot they were coming to take a statement from her.

"Kaymee Morrison, I am Officer Spencer and this is my partner, Officer Daniels. We need to ask you a couple of questions about what happened yesterday. Is that alright with you?"

Officer Spencer was an older guy that looked to be in his late fifties while Officer Daniels looked like a cold glass of ice water on a hot day. He was about six feet tall with a baldhead. He looked like the actor, Boris Kodjoe. I pried my eyes off the man so it wouldn't be noticeable that I was undressing him with my eyes. In my mind, he was already naked.

"Yes, that's fine," she responded, trying to sit up.

Standing to my feet, I helped her get in a sitting position while the older officer raised the head of the bed. When she was in a comfortable position, I sat back in the chair. She turned her head toward them and waited. He took a notepad out of his breast pocket and skimmed through it.

"Do you know who shot you, Miss Morrison?" Officer Spencer asked.

"No."

"There were witnesses that saw a woman and a man running away from the scene. Can you identify the suspects?" Officer Spencer asked.

"No."

"Some of the witnesses said there were words exchanged between you and the suspects. Do you remember what was said?" Officer Spencer asked.

"I don't recall saying anything to anyone but my dad," Kaymee responded.

Officer Daniels stepped forward with an irritated expression on his face. "Your father, Mr. Dawson, is upstairs fighting for his life. Are you going to keep sitting here acting as if you don't know what happened, Miss Morrison?"

Kaymee took a deep breath and held her head down. Her head snapped upright and she stared Officer Daniels in his face before she spit venom at him. "First of all, Officer Daniels, my daddy is not fighting for his life. Second of all, acting is the last thing I want to do in this situation. I can't act like I didn't get shot. That shit actually happened. Lastly, I want the person that shot me to get caught just as bad as you do, but I have nothing to give you. But I would appreciate if you would reframe from low key calling me a liar. I don't know what you want me to say, but I won't make up a story to make your dick hard. Now if you would leave, maybe I can get this arm set so I can go the fuck home."

Officer Spencer looked at his partner with disgust. I guess he didn't give the signal to play good cop, bad cop. Officer Daniels wasn't paying him any mind though, his glare aimed at Kaymee as she glared right back.

"Let's go, Daniels," Officer Spencer said, grabbing his partner by the arm. When he didn't budge, he repeated his demand louder.

"We will be paying you a visit really soon, Miss Morrison," Officer Daniels said snidely.

They left out of the door and the doctor and the anesthesiologist entered. The way that fine ass officer came at my friend pissed me off but she cut his ass deep. I was proud of the way she handled herself. Police were always trying to intimidate some damn body.

Dr. Reid walked over and stood next to the bed. "We will be in the operating room for a couple of hours. Are you ready?" he asked.

"Yes, I'm ready as I'm going to be," she said, turning to me. "Bestie, I want you to go home and get some sleep. Dr. Reid will call you and Mama Chris when I get out of surgery. I don't want you sitting around waiting for me."

I didn't want to leave her alone in this hospital, but she already told me what she wanted me to do. I had to oblige because if I didn't, it would give her something to worry about. That was something she didn't need to be doing at that moment. I wanted to go home to get my thoughts together to confront Monty. I couldn't let this shit linger too long because I didn't want him to think shit was sweet.

"Even though I don't want to, I will leave and I'll be back," I said to her. "Dr. Reid, look out for my sista. She means everything to me. I'm leaving her in your care. Don't make me have to come back and hurt you," I said, laughing but I was serious about what I'd said

"I promise nothing will happen to her. She is in good hands."

The anesthesiologist walked over to administer the medication needed to knock her ass out. When she started fighting to keep her eyes open, I started laughing because she was looking like a baby crackhead. I took that opportunity to gather my purse and phone.

"Okay, baby cakes. I'm out of here. I'm about to go home and brainstorm on the tattoo that you will be getting to cover that scar. I love you, sis," I said, kissing her on her forehead

"I love you too, Poe. Go talk to Monty and straighten that shit out before I beat y'all ass," she slurred before she closed her eyes.

Whatever was given to her knocked her ass out quick. I watched as her bed was rolled out of the room. I followed behind and went in the opposite direction to the elevator. While waiting for it to come, I went to the Lyft app and requested a ride. I had a fifteen-minute wait and that would give me enough time to blow something before I arrived at Monty's house. *I have to be high as fuck when I speak my mind*, I thought to myself as I got on the elevator.

When I arrived at Monty's house, I didn't expect to see his car in the driveway. I walked up the steps and unlocked the door, heading down the hall I noticed that Monty's door was opened, and he wasn't in there. I put my purse down and walked back out of the room to see where he was. Dray's door was closed but I heard the TV on, so I knew he was probably asleep.

## Meesha

His house wasn't that big, but it was big enough. I checked the kitchen and then the living room, but when I looked at the couch, I noticed that I had walked right past him when I came in. There was a bottle of white Hennessy opened on the coffee table with an ashtray full of blunt ducks beside it. I knew then that his ass was blasted. I left him right there and went back to his bedroom.

When I got in the room, I closed the door. Walking to the dresser, I grabbed a nightshirt and went to the bathroom to take a much-needed shower. The water relaxed my body to the point that I instantly got sleepy. Washing my body, I got out, wrapped myself in a towel, and went back to the bedroom. As I oiled my body with Aveeno lotion, my phone started ringing. I looked at the screen and it was a private call. Those were the calls that I didn't have time for. It wasn't anyone but I damn telemarketer. I let it go to the voicemail and crawled under the covers, closing my eyes I allowed sleep to take over my body.

## Chapter 9
### Dot

"Dot, won't you sit your ass down somewhere! You've been walking back and forth all damn night weighing down my damn carpet! And what I tell you about smoking them damn cigarettes in my house!"

I went over to my girl Yvette's house yesterday instead of going home. When I left the warehouse, I didn't look back to see if Stan was far enough away from that explosion. I hadn't heard anything about him dying, but I did know the car was found. It was burned completely and nothing was left of it except the body itself. That's why I wasn't too worried about the police going after him.

"How are you talking shit about me smoking when you smoke weed in this muthafucka? As for me walking back and forth, I have a lot on my mind right now. Can I think in peace, please?" I said, glaring at her with my hand on my hip.

"I can smoke whatever the hell I want in here because I'm the only person that pay to play where I lay. If you want to do what you want, go to your own house with that shit. You're running from something, Dot and I hope you don't bring your drama over here. I don't need all of that where I sleep at night."

This bitch had me all the way fucked up, talking to me like she had never done dirt with my black ass. Ever since she moved in this fancy ass house with the help of Section Eight, she thought she was better than me. Yvette could fool somebody that didn't know her ass, but I knew the truth.

"Bitch, are you acting brand new?" I asked her as I marched up to her. "I will slap the shit out of you, Yvette. Don't ever come for me when we were two peas in a pod before you moved out of the projects."

"Dot, get the fuck out of my face—."

She tried to jump bad and I did just what I said I would do. *Smack!*

She fell off the stool she was sitting on and rolled over on her side. I slapped her so hard, I had her saliva on my hand. Jumping up, she charged at me and I stuck the cigarette that I had in my hand under her eye.

"Aaaaaarrrggghh! Get the fuck out of my house and don't ever come back! I hope whatever you are running from catches your ass in the worse way! Get the fuck out!" she yelled, still holding her eye.

Since she wanted to continue to talk shit, I kicked her ass in her stomach and she doubled over. Grabbing her by her hair, I punched her in her face a couple times until her nose started leaking blood. I pushed her ass on the floor and took my time putting on my shoes, then I walked out without looking back.

I hurried down the street to the bus stop, getting there right on time because the bus had just pulled up. When I paid my fare and chose a seat in the middle of the bus, I started getting nervous. I was Kaymee's emergency contact and nobody from the hospital had called to say she was hurt. Maybe she was put in the system as a Jane Doe. I hoped that was the case because I didn't need that nigga Monty coming to fuck me up. He would be the first person she would call when she had the chance.

My stop was coming up and I stood after pulling the cord to alert the driver. Once the bus stopped, I got off from the back and looked around before I started walking toward my building. I looked at the time on my watch and it read five fifteen in the morning. The guys were outside the building as well as a couple crack heads like it was late evening or some shit. I walked pass them and went inside. I was tired as fuck. I walked back out of the building and approached the nigga that they called D.

"What up, Dot? What the hell you doing coming in this time of the morning? Where that fine ass daughter of yours at?" he asked me with a twinkle in his eye.

"Don't worry about what I'm doing out. I don't have a damn curfew. As far as my lil' bitch, I don't know where she is. When I see her, I'll make sure I hit you up so you can pay me to fuck her. Now give me three twenties and stay out of my business."

He went around the side of the building and came back with the weed I asked him for. I gave him sixty dollars and headed back inside the building to the elevator. The out of order sign was finally gone and I was glad about that. I sure didn't feel like walking up all of those stairs.

Unlocking the door to my apartment, I pushed it open and Stan was sitting on my couch with bloodshot eyes. He glared at me as if I killed his dog or something. I stood waiting for him to speak his mind, I didn't have time for bullshit because I was sleepy and ready to go to bed. He wasn't saying nothing and I wasn't feeling this standing shit.

"Stan, what are you doing sitting in my living room like you pay the bills in here? As a matter of fact, give me my damn key right now. You're posted up like you got it like that and you don't." I said, walking over to where he was sitting with my hand held out.

"Take this muthafuckin' key because after today, you won't have to worry about me coming back!" He took the key from his key ring and tossed it at my feet. "The police showed up at my house last night because they found my car burned up behind that warehouse. It's a good thing I reported it stolen after the bullshit you pulled! You ain't shit Dot and I don't know how I missed it!" he shouted at me.

I laughed at his ass because all I wanted was his dick. He should've left his eyes on more important shit. "You missed it because you had this kitty on your brain. How long have your ass been coming through here? Years, nigga! How didn't you notice that I didn't fuck with that bitch on any level? I don't even know how you're deep in your feelings over somebody you didn't even pay an ounce of attention to. Fuck you and yo' feelings. I don't care about you ever returning. I have plenty of men waiting for me to hit them up. I know one thing, though.

You better keep ya dick suckers closed about what happened or I a got a bullet with ya name on it, nigga."

I reached into my purse, pulled my gun out, and cocked it. I was ready to blow his ass away if he tried anything. "Now, get out and don't ever look back with your punk ass! The last thing I need is a soft muthafucka with a hard stick! You may as well have a pussy! Get out!"

"Dot, ain't no good gon' come to your ass and when you fall flat on your face, forget you ever met me!"

He walked to the door and I followed behind him. As he opened it and stepped out, I raised my foot and kicked him square in the ass. He turned around with his fists raised and lowered it slowly because he was met with the barrel of my gun. I thought his eyes would fall from the sockets. That's how big they were.

"I wish you would hit me. I promise you won't live to tell about it!"

"You got that. Your day is coming, Dot and I hope you get all that you deserve," he said, walking away.

I slammed the door and didn't have a care in the world. I did what I did and that was that. I went in my bedroom and grabbed a swisher off the dresser. I sat down and used my thumbnail to cut it open. Emptying the contents into the ashtray, I filled it with a hefty amount of the weed I had copped outside. Once I sealed it, I lit the blunt and hit it hard. Holding the smoke in my lungs for a few seconds, I blew it out. The taste that was in my mouth was one I had never tasted before when I smoked. The shit had me high as fuck off just one pull. It must've been some new shit. I didn't give a fuck, That shit was hitting right.

Finishing the blunt, I was so high that I fell back on the bed. I tried to sit up to hit it one more time and fell back a second time. When I finally sat up, I was having a hard time focusing. My vision was blurry and the left side of my face was numb. I was finally able to raise my arm to snub the duck out in the ashtray and I found myself nodding off. I struggled to kick my shoes off and laid back on the bed. Sleep took over before my head could settle on the mattress good.

Meesha

## Chapter 10
### Montez

The sun was beaming in my face and my back was stiff. I opened my left eye and noticed I wasn't in my bed. I was mad at myself because I barely allowed anybody to lounge on my couch, let alone sleep on it. Sitting up, my eyes went right to the coffee table. I had a mini smoke session by my damn self when I got home from the club.

Mena was wilding out and I still couldn't understand why. She knew what we had was about sex. Now she wanted to fuck up the rotation and make it out to be more. Her feelings were hers alone because mine didn't match. Slowly walking to my bedroom door, I grabbed the knob. My shoulders relaxed when I saw the sun kissing the side of my baby's face.

Moving quietly around the room, I got a fresh pair of boxers and a wife beater out of the drawer and went to take a shower. Hurrying to wash the events of the morning from my body, I didn't bother oiling up. Poetry's body wrapped in my arms was where I wanted to be and I wasn't about to prolong the wait. It hadn't been a full twenty-four hours, but I missed her.

Closing the door after I entered quietly, I walked to my side of the bed and crawled in. I placed my phone on the nightstand and before I could get in the bed good, my phone started ringing loudly. Poetry turned over and looked me in my face and I ignored the phone altogether.

"Good morning, baby," I said, leaning in to kiss her lips.

She turned her head and sat up still looking at me crazy. She finally got up and glanced around like she was looking for something. I felt like a damn fool for thinking she was going to sweep what happened yesterday under the rug. I bet she came over this morning to address the shit and I was passed out from all the weed I smoked. Sitting up and propping the pillow behind my back, I was ready for whatever she was dishing out. She was pacing back and forth in front of the bed with

Meesha

the most serious look on her face. I was about to say something
to her when my phone started ringing once again.

Her head snapped in my direction and I leaned over to see
who it was and, of course, it was Mena. Silencing the phone
and sitting back against the pillow, my phone ping with a text
and Poetry put her hand on her hip staring at me evilly. I didn't
want to add fuel to the fire but I wasn't answering that phone.
I said all I needed to say at the club.

My phone started ringing back to back for about five
minutes. Not one time did Poetry utter a vowel. She went from
her hand resting on her hip to folding her arms over her chest.
I didn't know what to do. Letting the phone continue to ring
without answering only pissed her off more.

"Okay, so who the fuck blowing your phone up early in
the fuckin' morning like it's an emergency? It's not about business because you're not scrabbling around this muthafucka trying to leave," she asked calmly. When I didn't reply, she huffed
and puffed turning her head looking away from me. Turning
back around, the tears in her eyes broke my heart. I wanted to
go to her and tell her how sorry I was.

"Did you sleep with her, Montez?"

Those five words were like hearing, "You have been sen-
tenced to life in prison". The only thing I could do was stare at
her as my own tears welled up in my eyes. At that point, I knew
I had to come clean. There was no point in lying. I let the air
that I had been holding in my lungs out. Pushing myself up off
the pillows, I swung my legs out of the bed and stood.

"Poe—" I said her name and that's as far as I got before
she cut me off.

"Montez, I'm not for the bullshit right now. I asked you a
question and it only requires a yes or a no answer. Let's try this
again. Did you sleep with her?" she asked the question again
but sternly.

My head dropped to my chest and the tears that I had been
holding at bay fell onto the carpeted floor. I raised my head
slowly and sniffed because my nose was trying to run. Taking

90

a couple of steps toward her, she held her hand up to stop me. I ignored her gesture and kept moving forward.

"Yes, I slept with her and I'm sorry, Poe. It was never supposed to happen. I made a mistake."

"It wasn't supposed to happen, but it did! Montez, I've been with you since I was fourteen and I've never thought of stepping out on our relationship, even when you were away at school! I don't want to think about how many hoes you have fucked around with in Atlanta and don't say none either. If you can shit on me in our hometown, I know damn well you were gettin' it in hundreds of miles away!" she screamed at me.

I took a few steps to get closer to her and touched her face. "I love you so much and I'm so sorry, Poe. She doesn't mean nothing to me," I all but pleaded.

She slapped my hand down from her face. "Yeah, I agree. You are one sorry excuse for a man. If this is the way that you love me, you can keep that shit. You will not get the chance to have me walking around looking like a muthafuckin' fool. I've given you every bit of respect and this is how you repay me? What happened to loving me for life, Montez? You said you wouldn't hurt me got dammit!"

She was crying and yelling and I felt the shit in my chest. I failed her and I knew it, something I promised I wouldn't do. "How can I make it right, baby? I don't want to lose you. It will never happen again." I reached out to hug her because her shoulders shook harder with every cry, but my phone started ringing as I gathered her in my arms.

Snatching away from my embrace, she stormed over to the nightstand and snatched the phone up. I took three long strides and snatched the phone out of her hand. I didn't need her to talk to Mena. I knew she was on bullshit and I already had to deal with Poetry and our relationship. If looks could kill, I would be dead the way she was glaring at me.

"How long have you been fucking the bitch from the club, Montez?" I knew it was more to it that day when you melted in her muthafuckin' arms in my face, nigga! You have history

91

with her ass and I'm giving you the opportunity to be straight up with me. Do not piss me off any more than you already have. I may be young, but I'm far from stupid!"

"I've known Mena for a couple years and yesterday was the first time I touched her, I swear. We're just friends, that's it," I said, looking away from her.

She chuckled, while shaking her head back and forth. "So, you're just gonna add insult to injury, huh? Do I look like boo boo the fool to you, Montez? You don't fuck your friends, nigga! Last week, that woman didn't have the look of friendship in her eyes. That was the I miss your dick look. It's the same way I look at your good for nothing ass when I lay eyes on you after you've been gone away to school, muthafucka! Don't insult my intelligence! You love me so much that you are willing to take this shit to the grave when I've given you the floor to come clean! Fuck you!"

Poetry rushed to the closet and grabbed her luggage. Snatching her clothes from hangers, she filled it to capacity. Before she could close it, I damn near ran over to where she stood and started taking the clothes back out. She wasn't about to leave me. What the fuck she thought? I didn't have shit to do, we could do this all day.

"Stop! I don't have time for you to act as if you want me to stay now, Montez! Would you please just let me leave? I'm not what you want. If I was, you would've controlled ya dick!"

I continued to toss her clothes out and tuned out what she was screaming. She pushed me with all of her might and I stumbled into the wall. I wanted to yoke her ass up because my lower back hit the corner of the wall, pinching a nerve. But I was wrong on all levels and I couldn't even begin to be upset. I was only trying to stop her from leaving because I wasn't letting her go that easily. She gathered her clothes off the floor and threw each item back into the luggage and I took them back out.

"You are pissing me off! Grow the fuck up and quit playing childish ass games! We are about to be fighting in a minute,

92

on my mama," she screamed, glaring at me. "It's all good! Keep that shit!" she said, yanking a pair of jeans from the floor putting them on.

She didn't bother taking her nightshirt off. She slipped her feet in a pair of Jordans and put her hair in a ponytail. As she grabbed her phone putting it in her purse, the doorbell rang. I didn't care who was at the door. Everybody knew not to show up at my house unannounced or they would be standing their ass out there until I gave them the okay to come over.

"Poetry Renee! You are not about to leave this house, ain't no breaking up! Another nigga won't be getting what's rightfully mine. You belong to me, we are about to talk this shit out, and then we will be good. I will apologize until I'm blue in the face if that's what it takes, but you will not be leaving like this."

"That's what you worried about, another nigga? You weren't thinking about me when you were balls deep in the next bitch! You sound stupid as fuck, Montez," she said, shaking her head. "Right about now, I don't care if you pass out in front of me. I'll call an ambulance on the way out! You can't make me stay! Now move out of my way!" she screamed directly in face.

I grabbed her by her shoulders and pried her purse out of her hand. It took a little bit of work because she had a strong grip on it. Bringing her hand up, she hit me.

*Pow!*

She punched me in my jaw and I had to will myself not to hit her ass back. I may raise my voice, but I have never put my hands on her. I wasn't about to start that day either. She had every right to be mad, but she was going to find a way to do that shit right in that room.

"Poe, keep yo' hands to yourself because if I hit you back, it's not gon' be nothing nice. This ain't us, baby. I'm sorry for what I did and you got me in here sounding like a bitch. That's how much I love you. I'm trying to right my wrong but you won't allow me to do that."

"You're sorry you got caught! Now give me my shit so I can go," she snarled.

There was a light knock on the door. Come in," I said, without taking my eyes off her. Her chest was heaving up and down, but I didn't care. She wasn't leaving. Dray stuck his head in, looking at both of us and shook his head. "What's up, fam?" I asked.

"Step out the room for a minute," he said, stepping back into the hall. I walked toward the door and Poe was right on my heels trying to get out the room.

"Poe, go sit down because you ain't getting out of this room."

"I'm about to go. I'm done with this shit, Montez. There's nothing else to talk about. You've said all I needed to hear. I love you, but obviously, it wasn't enough. We good, though. I don't hate you, but I can no longer be with you."

Hearing her say those words pissed me off to the max. "Sit the fuck down and wait 'til I come back! We will talk and you won't leave me over this shit!" I screamed in her face.

*Bam! Bam! Bam!*

"Who the fuck is banging on my fuckin' door, dude?" I turned, addressing Dray.

"That's what I want to talk to you about," he said, looking over my shoulder at Poe.

I didn't think anything of it, I demanded him to tell me what I was waiting to hear. "Well tell me, nigga. What the fuck you waiting for?"

"It's Mena—"

"Oh, is that right?" Poe asked sarcastically as she rushed past me.

I reacted too slowly because before I could get to her, she was snatching the door open. Mena was standing with her fists raised like she was about to knock again. I knew then shit was about to go from bad to worse. Mena still had on the clothes she wore to the club the night before and her eyes were bloodshot red. She was either high or had been crying all morning, maybe a mixture of both.

"Can I help you?" Poe asked too nicely.

"I'm here to talk to Montez," she said, trying to push her way inside but Poe blocked her from entering.

"Mena, right? Yeah, I remember you from the club. What's your relationship with him?"

"Come on, Poe—"

"Shut the fuck up, Monty! I'm not talking to you. I'm talking to ya bitch right now," she said without turning her head.

The look on Mena's face said it all. She didn't appreciate being called a bitch. "Who the hell are you calling a bitch? You got me messed up, lil' girl. To answer your question, I've been with Montez for the last two years. Yes, I knew all about your young ass, but I didn't give a fuck. I've been to Atlanta to see him and everything. When he comes home, he spends days with me without interruptions. You would call, but thinking back on it now, I would have to assume you didn't know he was back in the city those times. Don't ask questions you don't want the answers to," Mena replied with a smirk.

Poetry turned her head toward me and I knew it was over. She didn't cry, she didn't scream. She just walked toward me and stood there. As she did that, Mena came in and closed the door as if she was invited inside my shit. Before I could tell her to leave, Poetry slap the taste out of my mouth.

*Smack!*

I had gotten slapped twice in one muthafuckin' day, but this time, I deserved that shit.

"Two muthafuckin' years! Two years, Montez! You stood in there not even ten minutes ago, saying yesterday was the first time you slept with your *friend*," she said, pointing in the direction of my bedroom. "Just like I thought, you ain't shit! I will say this for the last time, I'm done. Don't call me, don't come to my house, and don't say shit to me when we get to Atlanta. I won't be the bitch that sit back and let you run over me. If I forgive you today, you will be between this bitch's legs again if the opportunity arises," she said, snatching her purse from my hand. "Bring my shit to my house and leave it on the porch."

She turned to go out the door and Mena stepped in front of her, halting her steps. "Didn't I tell you not to call me a bitch? I see you don't listen very well, huh, lil' girl."

I didn't know why the fuck Mena was trying to be messy. Poetry said what she said after the shit Mena revealed and didn't even say shit to her, but she wanted to egg the shit on. The outcome of this was not going to be a good one. Poetry didn't like when anyone stepped in her space.

"I called you a bitch and I would say it again, if the shoe fits. You and that nigga can continue doing what the fuck y'all want. I'm no longer an issue. You don't have to be his little secret anymore. Now you can fuck his ass on top of the John Hancock building in a split and I wouldn't give a fuck, but what you better do right now is get out my face! I had no intentions of saying shit to you beyond the question I asked. You answered it and I addressed the muthafucka I needed to address. You don't want to make this about you getting fucked up, Mena," she said, trying to move around her.

Mena wasn't trying to let her get to the door and I knew that Poe was only going to be calm for so long. I stepped up to defuse what I knew was about to happen but before I could get to Poe, she dropped her pursed and grabbed Mena by the front of her shirt.

*Wack!*

Poetry punched her in the face hard as fuck. Blood gushed out of her nose and her hands automatically went to her face.

"I tried to give your bitch ass a pass for the shit you were talking!"

*Whap!*

"But you wanted to push this young bitch. Now I have to show you that age ain't nothing but a number."

*Whap! Whap! Whap!*

96

"Choose your battles and be mindful of the muthafuckas you want to confront!"

*Whap!*

"Don't fuck with me and when you see me, bitch, cross the street because I'll always have a fist for you to chew on."

*Whap! Whap!*

I was trying to separate them. I had Poetry and Dray had Mena. Poetry was beating the hell out of that girl and she wasn't letting up. She was holding her shirt so tight that I couldn't get her hand open. Every time I tried to unclenched her hand, she hit Mena in the face.

"Poetry, let her go! This shit ain't even worth fighting for. That's enough," I said, still trying to stop her.

Dray yanked Mena by the waist and pulled her back. Poetry still had hold of her shirt and with Dray pulling on her, it ripped right off. She didn't have on a bra and her titties were out for everybody to see.

"Let me go! That bitch is about to get these hands!" Mena screamed struggling to get out of Dray's grip.

"If you saw your face, you wouldn't be talking about going in for round two. Take that L and let this shit die right here, ma," Dray said to Mena.

I was holding on to Poetry and she was trying to get at Mena. "Still talking shit, I see. There's more where that came from. Montez, let me the fuck go!" she yelled, hitting me in the mouth with her elbow. "Let her go, Dray! Square up, bitch!"

Letting her go slightly, I grabbed her arm again when I felt her moving in Mena's direction. My mouth was throbbing but I ignored, I would deal with it later. "There will be no more blows being thrown around this muthafucka today!" I managed to say through my bloodied lips.

Poetry shot me a look and bent down to retrieve her purse from the floor. Mena was still tussling with Dray trying to get at her. Dray had a tight grip on her waist trying his best not to touch her titties while he held her. She stomped on his foot, tried biting him, as well as scratching at his hands. None of the things she did fazed him at all.

"Don't worry, my practice session of boxing ended moments ago. I'm finished with this bullshit. I have better things I can do with my time and energy. Now you can nurse this bitch back to health. She may have a concussion," Poetry said, smirking.

"Watch your back, bitch! This shit ain't over!" Mena yelled as Poetry reached for the doorknob.

She turned to face her with a sinister smile on her face. "Before you come for me again, get your fight game up. Next time, I'm gonna fuck you up like the Russian did Apollo Creed in *Rocky IV*." Her head whipped in my direction and I was hoping she was about to say something like, "see you later" or "I love you", but none of those words fell from her lips.

"Don't forget to bring my shit to my house. After that, forget you every met me," she said, opening the door.

When she was almost outside, she rustled through her purse and pulled out her keys. She fumbled with them for a minute and turned around, throwing the house keys I gave her at my chest. Slamming the door behind her, she walked out of my life without looking back. It took everything in me not to run behind her, but I was willing to give her the time she needed to cool off. I still had to get this dizzy as bitch Mena out my shit.

## Chapter 11
### Kaymee

It had been two weeks since Jonathan and I was shot by Dot. I was in the hospital for a total of three days and I was glad when they finally let me go home. Dray and Monty came to pick me up, but Poetry stayed at the house and waited on my arrival. I was surprised when she came to see me when I got out of surgery and told me everything that happened, down to her whooping Mena's ass.

I was so mad at Monty and I let it be known when I talked to him. I cursed him out so badly that he hung up on me, but he called back after he realized that I was only speaking the truth. Finding out that he had that woman coming to see him in Atlanta is what had me thinking about what Dray was into as well at that point. We would have that conversation soon enough because I didn't want to walk into any mess when I went down south.

Poetry and I was sitting in the living room watching TV when her phone began to ring. She looked down at it and pressed the button to silence it. I knew it was Monty because she had been doing the same thing since she left his house that day. I didn't believe her at first when she said she was done, but she turned me into a believer with her actions.

"Would you answer his calls, sis? At least listen to what he has to say. He's been calling and coming over to see you and you just tell him to kiss your ass without saying it out loud. Y'all been together too long to let some broad come between y'all. I think he is truly sorry for what happened."

She looked at me like I had a booger on the tip of my nose. "I will not answer his calls and I don't give a fuck how many times he comes over. I will never be here! I don't give a damn if I'm sitting on the porch. I'm not home! That bitch didn't come between us. She didn't hold a gun to his head and make him fuck her for two damn years! You can sit back and have all the sympathy in the world for his ass, I won't. He did this all by himself, he's a grown ass man and he will eventually learn that I'm not to be played with. Now, enough about that, what are we getting into today?" she asked, turning her head back to the TV.

She read my ass and cut that subject short abruptly. There was nothing else I could say to convince her otherwise. "I wanted to go see Jonathan in the hospital. He is doing a lot better and he may be able to go home tomorrow. I'm so glad he pulled through and he will be good as new before long. I was so afraid I would lose him before I could get to truly know him, but prayers work and I'm glad God heard my cries. He is the only parent that I have left and I'm going to need him in my life."

"We can head to the hospital early but, we need to shop for the things we are gonna need for the dorm. I can't believe we will be in Atlanta next week attending Spelman! The college life is about to be lit. I can't wait. I get to experience this with my best friend, too!" she screamed, while kicking her feet in the air. "I know you don't want to talk about this, but have you heard from Dot?" she asked in a serious tone.

"No, I haven't heard anything from her. I was hoping Monty killed her ass, but when I asked him about it, he said they decided not to do anything to her until my dad was better. Other than that, I don't know where the hell she is and I don't care, actually. Getting away from here will be the best thing that has happened in my life, I can't wait to leave," I said lowly.

"Well, I know that big ass truck you got for your birthday will fit all of our shit and some. I'm glad we don't have to ride with Dray and his boy. Riding eleven hours with his ass would have killed me. I wouldn't be able to keep my mouth closed five minutes. That would be a long ass commute because we would be arguing the entire way.

I laughed because she was right. Both of them were head strong and never wanted to back down. Poetry usually ended all debates with him because she said he is the man and he should lead, but she refused to let him think he owned her.

Don't get me wrong, she stood up to his ass all the time, and got her point across, but she never disrespected him. I thought they would be together forever, but some things just don't work out that way.

"Well, let's get this day started. There's no time like now to get out and enjoy the day. It's almost noon anyway. Plus, we are already dressed to impress. Let's roll."

Standing from the couch, I glanced around looking for my makeshift scratcher I made from a wired hanger. My arm itched nonstop since I couldn't actually scratch it. Irritation was evident on my face because Poetry started laughing.

"You lost that damn gadget you made, huh?" she said, chuckling. "Look between the cushions. That was the last time I saw you with it."

I started snatching the pillows off and I didn't see it anywhere. "It's not here, sis! My arm is itching badly. Help me, please." I was ready to cry because my arm was itching like crazy and I needed that gadget to get to the itch.

All she was doing was clutching her stomach and laughing, pissing me off. I didn't see anything funny and I was ready to take this damn cast off any way I could. Poetry reached behind her back and pulled out what I was looking for. I wanted to club her with my cast. Instead, I snatched it and stuck it inside, relieving the itching sensation of my arm.

"You are over there scratching like a straight fiend right now, friend. Let me find out you got hooked on those meds they were giving you in the hospital," she said, laughing too hard for my liking.

"I advise you to stop teasing me. Break one of your limbs and let me know how that works out for your ass! You are being so irritating right now," I said with an entire attitude.

Leaving her ass there while she tried to get a slot on comedy central, I went to my room to grab my purse and keys. I was ready to get out of this house so I could focus on other things instead of getting upset. As I walked into the living room, my phone started ringing. I glanced at the screen and it was Monty. I already knew that he was trying to use me to talk to Poetry and I wasn't getting in the middle of that.

"Yes, brother," I said, answering the phone.

"Put Poe on the phone, Mee," he barked in a demanding tone.

"Monty, I'm not about to attempt to hand her this phone. How many times have you called her and she didn't answer? Please don't put me in the middle of y'all mess. This is between the two of you. Leave me out of it," I pleaded.

"I just want to talk to her. I'm trying to make things right."

"I understand that, but she doesn't want to talk to you. Monty, just give her time. I told you that when we talked. You're not giving her the opportunity to miss you," I said, trying to get him to see things my way.

"Why the fuck is you telling him that bullshit, bestie? I don't need time to miss his ass. I don't wanna talk to him. There's nothing for us to discuss. I made my decision and I'm sticking to it, plain and simple. Now, hang up the phone and let's go. I'll be outside waiting for you," she said, storming out the door, slamming it behind her.

I didn't know what to say to him from there. These were my two best friends and they were going to war with one another. Well, at least Poetry was at war with him. They were going to figure out how they were about to play this shit out, but I wasn't the middleman. I didn't want to see them apart, but it seemed as if Monty had to live with how it was about to be.

"I know damn well she didn't leave out without getting the phone!" he yelled. "Where are y'all about to go?

Telling him where we were going was something I wasn't revealing. That would be a disaster ready to happen. "Monty, we don't know where we're going yet. We're tired of being in this house," I said with a sigh.

"Yeah, a'ight. I'll hit you later to find out where y'all at. Tell ya friend that I'm tired of playing these fucking games with her. I won't wait forever," he said, ending the call.

The only thing I could do was throw my phone in my purse and head to the truck. When I got in on the passenger side of my truck, Poetry turned the radio up and threw it in reverse. She only did that so she wouldn't have to hear what I was about to say to her. Turning down the radio, I opened my mouth to speak and she started talking before I could.

"Don't tell me nothing that nigga had to say, Kaymee. It's over between us. There isn't going to be a second chance. I know how you are about the both of us and I hope you didn't tell him what we were doing today. I don't feel like arguing with him about his problem, especially not in public," she said, without taking her eyes off the road.

"Okay, I won't say anything about our conversation and I didn't tell him where we were headed because I don't want to deal with y'all shit either. I think y'all need to talk so there will be closure. If it's over, let that shit be known face to face."

"I told his ass all I had to say weeks ago. It was dead when I left out the door. Nothing else needs to be said. He chose to fuck the next bitch and continued to do so beyond the first time. If it was a one-time thing, maybe I could forgive him and talk it out but two years, Kaymee! Nah, I'm good."

"We drove in silence for a few minutes when my phone rang. A big smile appeared on my face when I saw Dray's name on the display. After securing my ear buds, I slid the button to the right to connect the call and put the phone in my lap. "Hey, babe," I said sweetly.

"What you up to, beautiful?" he asked nonchalantly.

"Poetry and I are spending the day out—" I stopped talking when I felt her elbow connect with my shoulder. I glanced to my left and was ready to snap when I saw her shaking her head no. I wasn't stupid. I knew that Monty put him up to calling me in order to find out where we were going. I rolled my eyes and continued my conversation. "Like I was saying, we are spending the day out to relax and enjoy ourselves. What do you have planned for the day?"

"Actually, I was hoping to spend some time with you Maybe I can meet up with y'all and the three of us can just hang for the day."

I knew I was right about his reason for calling. He may have wanted to spend time with me but Monty fucked that up trying to be slick. "Not today, baby. This day is for me and Poe, but I'll make it up to you. How does tomorrow sound? You can come pick me up early and we can spend the entire day together. How does that sound?"

"I wanted to spend today with you, though. Tomorrow seems so far away, Kaymee," he said.

"Dray, don't do this right now. I will spend the day with you tomorrow. Okay?"

He didn't answer, but I heard low murmurs in the background. I turned my head staring out the window trying to hear what was being said, but it was impossible to hear. "Dray, Dray, Dray! Are you still there?" I screamed into the phone.

"Yes, I'm still here. Have you changed your mind about telling me where you're headed?"

"No, I didn't and tell Monty to stop trying to use me to get to Poetry. That is foul as hell. He needs to give her space! I'm hanging up and I will call you later when I get back to the house." I didn't wait to hear his reply and hung up.

I couldn't believe Dray tried that stupid shit for his boy. I understood Monty wanted to talk to Poetry, but he was going about it all wrong. He needed to sit his ass back and let her cool off. Instead, he kept hounding her. It wasn't working, so he needed to lay low and be on his best behavior in order to get her attention again.

Pulling into the hospital garage, I got out once Poetry parked. We bypassed the information desk because we had passes already and showed them as we walked by. The elevator doors closed as soon as we rounded the corner. I pushed the button to summon another car and leaned against the wall.

"Kaymee, I will talk to Monty so we can end this the right way. I'm only doing this so he will stop hounding you. Other than that, it wouldn't take place."

The elevator opened and we stepped in. I pushed the number five button. "Don't talk to him because of me. Do it for yourself," I said, stepping out the elevator when we got to the fifth floor. Walking to my dad's room, his door was slightly opened. As I walked in, G was sitting in a chair by the side of the bed and a woman was sitting on the edge of the bed holding my dad's hand. My steps were slow at that point and I was wondering who the woman was.

"Hey, sweetheart. Come over here and give me a hug," my dad said, holding out his other hand.

I walked over, gave him a hug, and stood up straight. G got up and moved two chairs so Poetry and I could sit down. I couldn't take my eyes off the woman. I had to admit she was beautiful. She was light-skinned with long hair that was in loose curls that surrounded her face, her skin smooth, and blemish free. She looked young, but I wasn't going to assume her age because everyone knew black didn't crack.

"Baby girl, I'd like you to meet Katrina. She's my woman from Atlanta," he said, smiling.

I walked around to the other side of the bed and held out my hand for her to shake. Instead of shaking my hand, she stood and wrapped her arms around me. I hugged her back and for some reason, I felt a connection with this woman, and I didn't know who she was. Katrina pulled back, but her hands rested on my shoulders.

"You are so beautiful. Jonathan talks about you all the time and I couldn't wait to meet you. I heard you will be leaving for Atlanta to start at Spelman."

"Nice to meet you as well, Katrina. Yes, Poetry and I will be attending Spelman and I'm so excited," I said, glancing at my best friend.

Katrina turned her head and waved at Poe. "That's a very unique name. I love it. I'm ecstatic about getting to know you girls. We're all going to get to know each other together. I would be happy to show you girls around when we get back home to Atlanta.

"Slow down, Katrina," Poe said, laughing. "Thank you. I like my name, too. If you don't mind me asking, how old are you?"

"Since you asked, I'm forty-two, sweetie," she said, smiling and sitting back on the bed with my dad.

"You look good for your age and you seem cool and down to earth. I like you already," Poetry said.

"I agree with Poetry. We are gonna have so much fun." I was amazed because she didn't look like she was in her forties at all. Glancing in Jonathan's direction, I gave him the thumbs up sign and he laughed. I walked over to G and gave him a hug. "What's up, cousin? How's things going?" I asked as I sat down.

"Everything is cool on my end. I can't complain. I've been meaning to ask you, have you talked to your mama?"

"I haven't seen Dot since that day. Please don't talk her up. I was hoping she was mysteriously found floating in the Chicago River," I said with an attitude.

"Kaymee, I know what your mother did was foul, but killing her will not make the hurt go away," my dad said. "As bad as I want to shoot her between her eyes, she's not worth the bullet. Believe me, she was dead and gone last week, but I had a change of heart. Your mother will wish she'd never fucked with me when she starts to see her life fall apart right before her eyes. I won't have to kill her. She will kill herself."

"What do you mean by that?" I asked, sitting up in the chair.

"You said she don't work right?" I shook my head yes without saying anything. "She was living off the money you gave her every month and what I had been sending for years. I'm no longer sending her three thousand dollars a month and you haven't been giving her anything either. She doesn't have any source of income at all. She won't survive."

106

"Wait a minute, you mean to tell me that she was getting that much money and didn't spend a dime of it on me? I can't believe her good for nothing ass! I know that's not the plan you came up with. What else do you have? That's not going to make her life miserable. She has some guys that gives her a little bit of money sometimes," I scoffed.

"I have something in the works for her. I don't want you to worry about Dot. I have everything under control. Nobody gets away with fuckin' with me or my family. Remember that, baby girl. What do you have planned for the rest of your day? I know you're not going to sit here with your old man all day."

"No, I wanted to come and check on you before Poetry and I went shopping. We have to get some things for the dorm."

"Katrina, would you get my black card out of my wallet? This shopping trip is on me. Get everything y'all would need and anything you want. There's no limit to what you can buy. Shop until you're satisfied, both of you."

Katrina walked over and handed me the card and I just stared at it. I had never been given the opportunity of spending money freely. "I can't let you do that, dad. I have enough money to get the things that I need. Thank you, though," I said, getting up to give the card back to him.

"I know you can't *let* me do anything, but I insist. I've missed out on many years of your life and this is how I roll, baby girl. Get used to it. I have enough money for all of us to be good forever, the way you carry yourself, I know you would appreciate every dime of it. Money isn't going to bring you happiness, this I know. But I will try my best to keep a smile on your face from here on out. Go enjoy yourself and hold on to the card. I'll get it back when we get ready to leave for Atlanta."

"Poetry and I are driving ourselves down. We decided not to ride with Dray and Monty. I still haven't learned how to drive, so I couldn't drive that big ole truck you bought me," I said to him, shifting from one foot to the other.

"Don't worry. That's why Katrina is here. She's going to be the one to drive us back to Atlanta and now Poetry can help. How does that sound?" he asked with a smile on his face.

"Sounds good to me. It would give us an opportunity to get to know each other a lot better since that's a long ride," I said, giggling.

"You girls go ahead and have a good time shopping. I'll be getting out of here tomorrow morning. Maybe we can do dinner or something," he said, getting out of the bed.

All the while I had been in the room, I didn't pay attention to the fact that he didn't have any of the machines attached to him, not even an IV. His movements were back to normal, but I could tell he was still in a little bit of pain. Other than that, my daddy was going to be okay. I smiled with every step he took and welcomed him with opened arms.

When we broke the embrace, I looked at Katrina and she was smiling, too. "Would you like to go with us to shop on this old man's dime? Especially since he's adamant about me spending his money," I asked her with a smirk on my face.

"That's was so nice of you to ask, Kaymee. Hell yeah, I'll tag alone. Let's go put a dent in his wallet."

We all started laughing and I hugged my dad and G before turning to Poetry. "You ready to go, bestie?"

"You already know I am! Lead the way," she said, standing up. "See you guys later," she waved as we made our way to the door.

"Katrina," Jonathan called out. She turned around with love in her eyes as she glanced at him. "I love you, baby."

"I love you, too," she said, winking at him, leaving the room.

I knew then she wasn't one that was out for his money. The love between the two of them could be seen by Ray Charles himself. I was anxious to get to know her on a personal level, as well.

## Chapter 12
## Montez

I was getting tired of sniffing behind Poetry's ass just for her to keep blowing me off. The shit I did was wrong, but I only fucked up once. Damn, give a nigga a break. Apologizing and leaving Mena alone wasn't good enough. I'd been calling and going by her house every damn day for two weeks just to hear her mama or Kaymee say that she wasn't there. Shit, one time she was sitting right where I could see her and I was still told she wasn't home. That was that bullshit I was talking about.

When I called Mee and asked to speak to Poe, she wouldn't even give her the phone. She truly was not trying to fuck with the kid anymore. I wasn't giving up on what we had by a long shot. I even tried to get Dray to call Kaymee to see where she was headed and she didn't fall for the banana in the tailpipe. I called Poetry so many times that she eventually blocked me.

"Dray, do you have Mee's phone linked to your Find Friends app?"

He looked at me with a perplexed expression before asking, "Why?"

"Nigga, would you just answer the question, damn? You making shit complicated when you don't have to."

"Nah, correction. You are making things complicated. Give that woman time to think about if she wants to be with you or not, brah. Don't you see you are running her away? Y'all been together too long for her not to hear you out. One thing I do know is when time presents itself, you better tell her everything and don't leave nothing out. Mena shouldn't have been the one to tell her how long y'all were fuckin' around. That shit stabbed Poetry right in the heart because she gave you a chance to tell her."

"I didn't ask yo' soft ass shit about none of that! Are you following her or not?"

This muthafucka was trying to be a damn relationship therapist and his shit smelled worse than mine. I hope he had that

109

shit under control before next week or he would be in the same predicament I was currently in. With all the hoes he was fucking with at school, man, he better shut the hell up.

"Yeah, I follow her but don't expect me to go with you. I'm not trying to be in that shit. I already got my ass bit, scratched, and stomped on for you, nigga," he said.

"A'ight, cool. Let's go. Where they at?" I asked, grabbing my keys.

"Didn't you hear me when I said I wasn't going, Monty?" he asked, mean mugging me.

"I heard you, but I wasn't trying to hear the bullshit. Now let's ride, the only way I can keep track is with yo' phone, jug head."

I left out of my crib and walked to my car, hitting the unlock button before I got to it. Starting the car, I connected my phone to the Bluetooth and it started ringing. I looked at the radio display and it was Mena. Her ass just wasn't giving up. Things should've already registered in her head that we were done. It had been weeks since I'd talked to her and she wasn't going to get me to answer her calls any time soon.

Letting the call continue to ring, I took a blunt out of the armrest and blazed up. I glanced up through the hazy smoke and Dray still hadn't emerged from the crib. I picked my phone up to call him as I took another puff and he walked out and locked up. He must've known that I was about to go in on his ass if I would've had to call him.

When he got into the passenger seat, I put the car in reverse and pulled out of the driveway. "Where are we going, brah?"

He looked down at his phone and hit a couple of buttons. "They are at Oakbrook Center mall," he said, placing the phone in his lap.

"Why the hell did they go all the way out there? All the malls that are closer and they go to bumfuck Egypt to spend money," I said, gripping the steering wheel tightly.

Traffic was heavy and I hated sitting in wait. We had been on the road about twenty minutes and they could be anywhere by the time I made it to the mall. "Are they still at the mall?" I asked, scrolling through my phone for something to listen to on the radio. We had been sitting in the same spot for about ten minutes.

"Yeah, they're still there. This traffic is a muthafucka. You should find an alternate route, brah."

"Going in the direction that we're going at this time of the day, all roads look like this. It's called rush hour."

I was just as irritated as he was at that moment. The traffic started moving at a steady pace after about ten minutes. Getting closer to the mall, I was getting kind of nervous about sneaking up on the girls. This had to be done because I had never been in the shadows of my girl. I was always the next in line after her family. I haven't been a thought in her mind for weeks and it wasn't sitting well with my heart.

Finding a spot outside the mall, I got out and headed to the entrance with Dray behind me. We followed the dot on his phone and found the girls inside the Apple store. There was a woman that I didn't recognize with them and I didn't want to barge in on her just yet. Both Kaymee and Poetry were looking at MacBooks. I was going to buy them each one for the upcoming school year but it seemed as if I wouldn't have to.

They selected their computers with the accessories they wanted and were making their way out of the store. We ducked off into the store next door until they passed by. I let them get some ways ahead and then followed behind them at a safe distance. Poetry was looking good as fuck in the damaged jeans she was wearing and the cute shirt that showed off her toned arms and back. I guess I wasn't' the only one that was admiring her beauty because this dude walked up to her and didn't waste any time sparking a conversation.

My blood started boiling over like a pot of grits. Dray grabbed my arm when I moved toward them fast. "Aye, man. This is not the place to make a scene," he said, trying to reassure me.

Snatching my arm out of his grasp, I stormed over to where they were standing. Poetry was smiling like a Cheshire cat and that did something to me. She was giving that muthafucka the impression that he had a chance but wouldn't even answer my calls. Nah, that shit was not about to go down the way she thought it would. I stormed toward them full speed.

"How can I get to know you, cutie?" I heard the dude asked, while licking his lips.

"You can't," I said, putting my arm around her shoulders. "She got a man, brah. Go find you another bad bitch to push up on. This one ain't it."

"My bad, homie. I didn't know she was taken. You got a beauty on yo' arm. Hold on tight," he said, back peddling while still ogling my girl. I wanted to punch his ass for being cocky. Poetry didn't waste any time giving me a piece of her mind.

"What the hell is your problem, Montez? We are not together, so how dare you try to stop me from getting to know someone else! You are the one that turned what we had to shit, not me! I knew what I wanted when I committed to you. It was your decision to go outside of us to get some pussy! It didn't look too good to see someone interested in me, huh? Yeah, that's not even half of how I felt when I found out what you did. For the last time, stay away from me," she demanded as she stomped away to catch up with Kaymee.

Watching her walk away without giving me the chance to really talk to her had a nigga in his feelings. I didn't leave the mall. We walked around and shop a little to keep my mind off what was going on with Poe. After a while, we decided to get something to eat. I got in line at Chipotle and decided to order a burrito bowl. As I waited on my food, I turned and looked out into the seating area to see if there was any tables available close by. I spotted Mee and the mysterious woman, but I didn't see Poe with them. I continued to scan the area and my eyes landed on the same dude sitting with my girl laughing and giggling like a happy couple.

112

The first thing that came to mind was that Poetry thought I was a fucking joke. Before I could think about what I was going to do, I found myself rushing in their direction. I could hear Dray calling behind me loudly but Poetry didn't. She was so into whatever dude was saying that she didn't know I was almost right on top of her.

"Poetry I see you think I'm a joke! What the fuck did I say before? You are not on the market, you are far from single, and you will not talk to no other fuckin' niggas. I will blow this muthafucka's head off just to let you know how serious I am today!"

She sat there bucked eyed and didn't know what to say. I looked between the two of them and ole boy had a smirk on his face as if he wasn't bothered by what the fuck I said. "Look, man. It's not that serious over a bitch."

I tried to knock his head off when he disrespected her by calling her a bitch. Punching him over and over in his face, I saw the blood gushing out of his left eye. His mouth and nose were bruised up, too. When he fell out of the chair, I jumped on top of him and took my tool off my waist. I place the barrel under his chin and he started rambling like a toddler.

"I—I—I apologize, man. Don't shoot me!" he cried out.

"I'll kill yo' muthafuckin' ass, nigga," I said, hitting him over the head with my piece. His head burst open and I knew he would need a ton of stitches to close that gash. "You should've took heed to what the fuck I told you earlier. That's what your bitch ass get for lowkey saying fuck me. This is what I do to disrespectful ass niggas. I bet the next time you try to holla at a female you will make sure she's single."

Dray ran up and grabbed me off the dude, pushing me toward the nearest exit. "What the fuck is your problem, brah? That was some reckless shit you did back there! Do you think what you did back there is gon' make her come back to you? It was stupid on your part, brah!"

"Fuck that shit! I told that nigga that she was not looking for any new muthafuckin' friends! Poetry better get ready because every nigga I see in her face gon' get his ass beat! She'd better stop trying me like I'm some soft ass nigga. I'm done playing these fucked up games. I'm ready to body plenty niggas, believe that!"

I was halfway out of the mall when I heard Kaymee yelling for me to stop. Pushing the door open, I kept moving because arguing with her was not on my list of things to do. "I know your ass hear me calling you. That shit was wrong for real, brah. Why would you come here and embarrass her like that? How did you know where we were anyway?"

She was throwing questions at me faster than a kid skipping rocks in a pond, but I didn't slow down until I felt her tug on the back of my shirt. I swirled around and we were face to face. Her eyes were puffy and her nose were red. I knew then that she had been crying.

"The fuck you crying for? To answer your question, I didn't embarrass her. She embarrassed her damn self. Y'all seem to not understand that I gave that punk ass nigga a warning the first time. He was the one that came and took another shot at what's mine! Poe will learn sooner than later that I can do this shit and never get tired.

"It's not even worth all that you're doing right now! You did this shit, Monty! You were the one that stepped out on y'all relationship, not the other way around. If you thought you lost her then, you definitely lost her now. She doesn't ever want to see you again and I don't blame her!" she said, turning around to walk away.

"It's gon' be alright, baby. Finish shopping and I'll see you later. Call me when you get home and I'll come scoop you up. I'm about to get this nigga away from here so he won't get in trouble," Dray said, gathering her in his arms.

"I told you that I will hang out with you tomorrow. You shouldn't have come with him, Dray. I'm still curious to know how y'all knew where we were. This was the reason we came all the way out here in the first place." She pulled away glancing up at him, then took her phone out of her purse. Tapping a few buttons, she shook her head and chuckled. "Don't set him up to fail again. Now you can't track my movements anymore. Stay out of their relationship. It's not your battle to fight," she said, leaving his ass standing there looking stupid.

"Let's go before I follow my inner mind to go back in there and kill that nigga," I said, hitting the alarm on my ride so I could head back to the crib.

Meesha

## Chapter 13
### Kaymee

I was so mad at Dray that I didn't say anything to him for two days. Using my phone to track my location was stupid on his part. He let Monty talk him into doing that shit and look what happened. That man got his ass beat because of Monty's hot-headed ass. He needed to stop and realize threatening to kill people was not going to get Poetry to forgive him.

When he called for the umpteenth time, I decided to go spend some time with him. I couldn't even front, I was missing him, but I wasn't fully over what he did. He suggested Great America as the outing for the day. I was excited because I had never been to an amusement park a day in my life. Hell, I hadn't been anywhere until I met Poetry and Monty and that was limited because Dot wouldn't allow me to have fun.

"Oh, wow! Look at that big ass rollercoaster!" I said, getting out of the car after Dray parked the car.

"You want to get on that?" he asked once I was standing beside him.

"Hell nawl, I'm gonna eat while you ride. I don't think I can get on these rides, Dray. The way my heart is setup I'm not gonna be able to do it."

He hit me with the side eye looking across the parking lot. Turning back to face me he asked, "Why are we here, baby? I'm not about to pay fifty-four dollars for you to spend more money just to eat. We came to have fun and the shit you are trying to do, we could've done back at Monty's crib. Plus, you have never even been on a rollercoaster before, so how you know you won't like it?"

Glancing back at the rollercoaster, I was nervous, but he was right. I didn't know how I would react to the rides. Besides, it took us forever getting all the way out there with traf-fic. Taking my phone out of my fanny pack, I took a picture of the parking sign so we would know where we parked. We were in Group C4. I placed my hand in his and started walking

"Anything for you, baby. I will try my best to keep a smile on your face. You deserve it. Are you ready to play these games so I can kick yo' ass?"

"You didn't learn shit at Dave and Busters, huh? Let's get it, playa," I said, rising up from the seat.

We played a lot of games and it was a split down the middle as far as who won. He won some and so did I. I had so many teddy bears that I started giving them to random kids. The giant Tweety Bird and Snoopy were the ones I kept for myself.

"Let's get out of here, It's gon' be hell getting out of the parking lot. I'm so tired, but I had fun today."

"Me too! I don't think I've had this much fun, ever! I'm tired, as well. I hope you don't get mad if I get in the car and fall asleep on your ass," I said, laughing.

He switched the picture we took together in his right hand and grabbed mine with his left. Bringing it to his lips, he kissed the back of my hand. I turned to look into his eyes and he bent down kissing my lips deeply. I snaked my tongue into his mouth and he welcomed it with ease.

I couldn't believe I was standing in the middle of an amusement park molesting this man's mouth. My actions surprised me because all of a sudden, my kitty started purring like never before. The thoughts in my mind instantaneously went to him easing into my wet tunnel. I broke the kiss and held my head down blushing. Never letting my hand go, he licked his lips and led me toward the exit.

I didn't know how long it took to get out of that parking lot. All I know is, I was knocked out before we did. The events of the day were dancing behind my eyelids and I was reliving ever moment of it. Before long, I was being nudged by Dray.

"Come on, bae. We are at the house."

Hearing his words, I couldn't open my eyes to respond nor react to what he was saying. My body had a mind of its own because I couldn't move a muscle. It felt like a bitch had jetlag and I hadn't even been on a plane.

"Kaymee, wake up, baby. I'm too tired to carry you."

I was trying my best to wake up but every attempt was an epic fail. Now I knew what it felt like for a toddler when they played themselves to death at Chucky Cheese. When I felt his hand massaging my bud through my pants, my body started waking up slowly, but my mind was not communicating with it.

"Mmmmm," is what I heard come from my lips. Letting him play in my twat while sitting in the car was something I wasn't about to let happen. My head rolled to the side and I looked at him through half opened eyes. He rubbed harder and my hips gyrated against his hand. I grabbed it and sat up. "Okay, I'm awake."

"I knew that would get you up. She's ready for me. You won't be able to stop her from talking to me much longer." He winked at me and got out of the car.

My body was screaming from his touch. Before I got out of the car, I had already made up my mind that I was giving up the goodies that night. The ache in my pants was one that needed to be taken care of. I grabbed my prizes and got out of the car.

Dray was standing at the door waiting for me as I climbed the stairs. The way he was staring at me only made the moisture between my legs flow effortless. This feeling was new to me and I was nervous as hell. Entering the house, the aroma of weed hit me in my face.

As I stepped deeper into the house, I saw Monty sitting back on the couch. There was a fifth of Hennessy and three blunts sitting on the coffee table. He had two roaches sitting in the ashtray and a half full glass of liquor next to it. I walked to the couch and sat next to him.

"You good, fam?" Dray asked with his hand on his shoulder.

Monty nodded his head yeah but he didn't say anything else. I looked up at Dray and he hunched his shoulders. "I'll be in there in a minute. Let me talk to bro for a minute."

121

He nodded and walked down the hall to the bedroom. I sat looking at the side of Monty's face a few minutes before speaking. "Are you okay, bro? I can just imagine how long you've been sitting her drinking and smoking your life away."

When he looked at me, his eyes were bloodshot red and puffy. I had never seen him in this state before. Without responding to me, he picked up the glass of liquor and I snatched it out of his hand. The way he was looking, he had his fair share of alcohol, and I wasn't about to sit back and watch him continue the shit.

"What, Mee! Hell nawl, I'm not okay! I lost my muthafuckin' girl, man!" he screamed.

"So, you're gonna sit here and drink your life away? How's that going to make things better?" I asked.

"It may not make shit better, but it's numbing the way I'm feeling right now. I know I messed up, but why won't she talk to me? I love her ass, Mee! That nigga was dead the other day if Dray hadn't pulled me off his ass. This shit is driving me crazy. You better tell yo' girl that I'm murking all niggas that look like they about to step to her," he slurred.

He sounded like a damn fool, but I knew it was the alcohol talking crazy, not him. I screwed the top back on the bottle and stood up with it in hand. I walked behind the couch to the kitchen and his eyes followed every step I took.

"Bring my shit back, sis! I'm not finished drinking!" he yelled to my back.

I ignored the fuck out of him. He's lucky I didn't pour it down the drain, but I knew I would have to buy him another bottle if I did. "You better puff, puff pass by your damn self because all you will be drinking is water until you pass out. There's still a little bit in the glass in front of you. Sip on that slowly!" I yelled from the kitchen.

I put the bottle behind the microwave and opened the refrigerator, retrieving two bottles of water. Assuming he hadn't eaten, I made two turkey sandwiches with lettuce, tomato, mayo, and cheese. I put the food on a plate and grabbed a big bag of plain potato chips and the water. Placing all of the items on a tray, I headed back to the living room.

"Here, eat this and here's your water. I'm going to spend some quality time with my man. I'd advise you to sleep that alcohol off. You may not remember this in the morning but Poetry needs time, bro. You cheated on her and you want her to just forget about it and jump back in like nothing happened. It doesn't work that way. She is a different type of woman. She gave you her all for four years, and to find out that you were fucking someone on the side for two. How do you expect her to feel? You brought this on yourself. Now leave her be for a while."

I got up but I never took my eyes off of him. The words I spoke were true and he needed to hear them. I knew he was hurting, but he couldn't blame anyone but himself. I walked in front of him past the coffee table and noticed his car keys. Scooping them up, I held them in my hand as I glanced at him. "You won't be needing these in case you get any bright ideas during the night," I said and smirked, walking down the hall.

"Mee!" he yelled out. Turning to face him, I waited for him to speak. "You ain't my damn mama, but thanks for looking out for a nigga. I love you."

"I love you, too," I said, leaving him sitting there alone.

Meesha

## Chapter 14
### Drayton

When Kaymee and I walked into the crib, the weed smoke greeted us with a smooth hello. I knew my nigga was loaded before I even laid eyes on him. Once he told me that he was good, I went to the bedroom because just like Monty was protective of her, she was just as protective of him, too. I knew that she was about to go in on his ass and I didn't want no parts of it.

Hearing my baby tell him what he wasn't seeing was real shit. It was good that he was kind of listening to what she was saying because I didn't want him to do anything he would regret. Like Kaymee said, he needed to give Poe time to think about the situation and also to miss his ass. If he kept harassing her, he was going to lose her.

I grabbed some clean boxers and a white tee and headed to the bathroom to shower. As I walked out of the room, Kaymee was walking down the hall toward the room. She winked her eye at me and kept stepping. Blowing a kiss at her, I went into the bathroom and closed the door.

After the door closed behind me, I had a strong urge to piss. I took off my clothes, walked to the toilet, and drained the weasel. It felt like I had been standing there for the longest time, but it wasn't even an entire minute. Shaking him off, I turned the shower on and hopped in after flushing.

Closing my eyes as the water hit every muscle in my body, the image of Kaymee's ass invaded my thoughts. It was time for me to get into something tight and wet. I hadn't gone without sex this long ever. I was tired of beating the fuck out of my Johnson. Something had to give immediately.

I washed my body and got out. The urge to jack was at the forefront of my mind, but I didn't do it. I knew what the fuck I wanted and it didn't have anything to do with my dick in my hand. After drying off, I threw the tee over my head and stepped in my boxers. I opened the door and Kaymee was standing there with a shocked expression on her face.

"Oh shit, you scared me. I was just waiting on you to finish so I could take a shower," she explained without me saying anything.

In my mind, I wondered if she was contemplating joining me in there. I was kicking myself for not staying in longer. "My bad, baby. I'm finished in here, though. It's all yours. Something tells me that you wanted to come in before I was done."

Her face turned beet red. I smirked at her and kissed her on the cheek. Walking away, I had a feeling that I was being watched. I turned and looked behind me and sure enough, my baby was lusting like a muthafucka while licking her lips. When she noticed I caught her, she scrambled into the bathroom and slammed the door. I laughed all the way to the room. She was something else.

She stayed in the bathroom for damn near an hour. I got in bed minus the shirt and boxers, and turned on the TV to wait on her. The way she looked at me in the hall, there was no way she wasn't trying to let me pop that cherry. But if she didn't, that was fine, too. But I would be tasting that shit at least.

The door crept open and she peeked in. The light from the TV didn't help her none. I knew then that she was trying to figure out if I was still awake. I didn't move an inch, but I was looking directly at her with my arms behind my head. The way she was tiptoeing into the room almost made me laugh out loud. She closed the door quietly and walked over to the bed.

Easing into the bed, she turned her back to me and laid there. I wanted to see what her next move would be, so I waited. She turned over and I closed my eyes quickly because I wanted to see how things were about to play out. She sighed deeply and moved a little, resting back on the mattress. A few seconds later, I heard her talking lowly.

I peeped through my lids to see what she was doing and she was on the fuckin' phone. I wondered who the hell she was talking to at two in the morning. I wasn't left in the dark for long once I tuned in to what she was saying.

"Poe, you have to help me make a decision. He was looking so good when he came out of the bathroom. My kitty is tingling and I don't know what to do!" she whispered into the phone. I guess Poetry was coaching her on what to do about her situation because she was quiet for a moment.

"He's sleeping but I know he don't have on a shirt. I don't know about his boxers," she whispered again.

I closed my eyes again when I felt the bed shift with her movements. Lifting the covers, she used her phone for lighting, "Oh my god!" she gasped and turned back over fast as hell. It was hard as fuck for me not to laugh, but this shit was hilarious. I was able to compose my laughter, not wanting to embarrass her.

"Poe, his dick is big as fuck! Hell nawl, he ain't puttimg all that in me! That shit is gonna hurt," she said a tad bit louder.

She had every right to be scared of what I was packing. My nine-inch dude wasn't nothing to fuck around with, so I wouldn't even be mad if she chickened out after the shit I was witnessing. I could hear Poetry going in on her ass, but I couldn't make out what was being said.

"Okay, okay. I'll do it. My clit is hurting and I want it to stop. You promise it won't hurt that bad," she whispered.

Poetry was giving her an earful and I was happy she called her. I was going to have to buy her a fuck gift or something because she just answered a nigga's prayer. I owed her ass big time for this shit.

"Okay, I'm about to get off this phone and get my nerves together to initiate this. I'll call you in the morning. Thanks, bestie. I owe you one. Pray for me," she said, ending the call.

I acted like I was getting comfortable and turned over facing her, my eyes were still closed and I evened my breathing out to make it seem like I was sleeping. She reached over, placed her phone back on the nightstand, and turned in my direction.

Feeling her hand outlining my eyebrow, I was confused because not one woman had ever done that to me. It was different. Next, she ran her finger along my jawline as if she was trying to sculpture my face or something. She then moved closer to me and kissed my lips softly. At that moment I let my eyes flutter open like she woke me.

"Hey, beautiful. You finally decided to come to bed, huh?" I asked, smiling.

"Yeah, I couldn't hide out in the bathroom all night. I um, want you to do something for me."

"What would that be?" I asked as if I didn't already know.

She hesitated for a few seconds then she kissed me again and grabbed my hand, putting it under the t-shirt she was wearing. When my hand connected to her mound, I let my fingers do the talking. I strummed on her bud and it was already hard and ready. She was sloppy wet and I had just begun.

"Mmmm, she's ready for me, huh? Are you sure you're ready for this, baby?" I asked lowly. I stuck my middle finger inside her sweet tunnel.

"Mmmmhmm," she moaned with her eyes closed.

I knew I had to play around inside of her with my finger for a bit, so I was taking my time with her. When I was done, she would be overly satisfied feinin' for the lovin'. Rising up, I made my way between her legs. I was face to face with her pussy. My mouth started watering like I was starving and I was about to feast on a gourmet meal.

She grabbed the back of my head and slightly pushed it forward. This was something that she was familiar with. She knew what this tongue could do and she wanted it. I let her guide my head to her treasure and I covered it with my mouth.

"Oooouuuu, shit," she moaned.

I licked every inch of her kitty before I wrapped my lips around her bud. As soon as I clamped down on it and sucked, she was gyrating against my mouth. My finger was still deep inside her and she was fucking the shit out of it. I took that opportunity to insert my index finger, she didn't notice at all. It actually made her buck against my fingers.

My fingers were pretty long, so it didn't take much to find her G-spot. I pressed it with both of my fingers and she screamed out, "What are you doing to me?" Reaching above her head, I snatched a pillow and put it over her face to muffle her cries. I didn't have any plans of stopping.

Her walls tightened around my fingers and her thrust became faster. I got on my knees and sucked on her clit harder. Her breathing became labored and I knew she was on the brink of exploding. I could taste the nectar in my mouth, but I wanted the waterfall. I gave her bud a couple of plucks with my tongue and grasped it strongly with my lips. Her hips elevated and the rain came pouring down and I drank every drop.

Wiping my mouth with my hand, I eased my fingers out while watching her chest heave up and down rapidly. I snaked up her body, kissing my way from her kitty to her breast. I paid both of them ample amount of attention before I lifted the pillow and stuck my tongue in her mouth. Our tongues did a tango while I continued to finger her twat.

I grabbed my man while kissing her and put the tip at her door. She tensed up once she realized what was happening. "Relax, baby. Do you trust me?" I asked, looking in her eyes. She nodded her head yes and I proceeded to enter her sacred spot.

"Aaargggh! Dray, it hurts!" she yelled out, biting my shoulder.

She could do whatever the fuck she wanted at that point, because I was already in. I didn't care. I'd deal with the wounds later. I wasn't even all the way in and I felt my nut trying to make an appearance. That shit wasn't about to fuck this up for me. As tight as she was, I had to come to a complete stop to get my mind right.

I started moving in and out of her honey pot slowly. She was wet as hell, so my lil' dude was gliding with ease. She still wasn't moving with me but I was almost completely in. I thrust a little more and she shrieked in my ear, "It burns, baby! Take it out! Take out! I can't take it."

"Kaymee, baby. If I take it out, we will have to start over. Relax for me, baby. I'm almost all the way in," I said, thrusting slowing as I pushed a little bit more in.

"Oh shit! That feels good! Keep doing that," she moaned.

It was on from that point. I lifted her leg a little bit so I could have all access to that ass. I got a rhythm going and it was over for her. I had all nine inches inside, tearing her guts up. The way she was moaning and clawing at my back, I knew she was enjoying every minute of my dick. My back burned with every scratch she made.

"Oh, my God. Why do I feel you in my stomach? Yes, baby! I love you so much!" she screamed out.

The fuck faces she was making was pushing me to the edge because the sight before me was sexy as hell. The way her titties were bouncing with every stroke automatically made me take one of her nipples in my mouth. That's what brought her to her peak. Her tight walls were hugging my joint and I felt her juices spilling out all over the bed and my thighs.

"I'm cummin', Dray! Fuck, baby!" she screamed.

She had a death grip on my shit and I was about to pop my lid. Sitting up on my knees, I stroked two more times and snatched out, cummin' all over her titties and her stomach.

"Aaaaaargggggghhh! Grrrrrrr! Damn, baby! Yeah, aaaaaaaaaah" I growled before I collapsed on my side, avoiding falling on top of her.

Love Shouldn't Hurt 2

## Chapter 15
### Poetry

I hadn't wanted to do much of anything since everything transpired between Monty and I. Blocking him from calling was one of the hardest things I've had to do in a long time. His actions at the mall that day only pissed me off more. He had some nerve getting mad because another muthafucka had interest in something he took for granted. He needed to realize that he wasn't going to be able to pull a gun on every nigga that came at me.

He was the one that broke us up when he laid down with that bitch. I didn't have shit to do with it. I wasn't there holding his dick guiding it inside her messy ass. That was his choice to make. I gave him the opportunity to tell me the truth and he still lied. I shouldn't have heard the shit from her. He should've told me!

But nah, he wanted to take that shit to the grave and I was never supposed to find out. It made me think about how many times he had laid up with her and came to me, kissing me in my fuckin' mouth. The shit turned my stomach. Yeah, I was deep in my feelings and my music of choice told it all.

"In My Feelings" remake just so happened to come on Pandora while I was laid up listening to music and it's been on repeat ever since. This song had all my emotions and thoughts in one track. And it expressed what was going through my head to the T.

*I'm drained, physically, mentally, emotionally*
*I done gave you all of me but still you couldn't devote to me.*

I laughed to myself because that right there, yeah, I felt that shit! I gave his ass all of me and some but that didn't stop him from going to the next one. I was trying not to cry because I knew I was good to his ass the entire time, it just wasn't enough. But that's the type of female I was. I was loyal as fuck and still got the ass end of the stick.

*Just let me go leave me alone*
*You know damn well*
*You doing me wrong*
*You know damn well I don't deserve all*
*The shit that you do*
*But you still blowing up my phone like*
*"Bae, wait don't walk out."*
*"Bae, sit down let's talk about it."*
*"Baby, don't leave just think about it."*
*And then I tweaked about it.*

If this song is not telling me what I'm currently going through, somebody needs to slap the fuck out of me. Monty sounded just like this when he left messages on my phone and I got tired of hearing that shit. It was the reason he got blocked, but I've been fighting the urge to call him. I missed him so much but I couldn't let him think everything was good when it wasn't.

*What did I do to deserve all this pain?*
*Gave you loyalty and all I wanted was the same*
*Gave you all my trust*
*But you took that shit in vain*
*Tried to play me like a goofy*
*Like I didn't know the game*
*But, I'm done nigga*
*I'm done wit you...this my message*
*From me to you*

And just like that, from listening to a song fifty eleven times, I was sticking to my decision to leave Monty alone for good. The tears that I had been holding in for the longest finally won the battle and fell from my eyes. Trying to be strong while my heart was broken in a zillion pieces was not an easy task. Pretending to be all right when you're not was even harder.

Smiling and laughing around my parents took a lot of work. Now that I was in my bedroom by myself, everything I held in came out. I cried so much that I went to sleep without knowing because that was the only way I could stop my head from hurting.

I was awakened from my sleep around two in the morning because my phone started ringing. My first thought was that Monty was calling from another number. I wasn't going to answer at first but I had to remember that Dot's stupid ass was still breathing. Whoever was on the other end must've really needed to talk to me.

Reaching under the pillow and snatching the phone, I saw Kaymee's name on the display. I hurried to answer the phone before it went to voicemail. "Best friend, what's wrong?" I automatically said into the phone.

"Poe, you have to help me make a decision. He was looking so good when he came out of bathroom. My kitty is tingling and I don't know what to do!" she whispered into the phone.

I started laughing my ass off and didn't mean to. My boo was scared as hell of getting the dick that she obviously wanted. I had to take a few breaths to calm myself down before talking to her.

"Hold on, you calling me before you make a move on the brother. What is he doing while you are on the phone with me? Do he have on any clothes?"

"He is sleeping, but I know he don't have on a shirt. I don't know about his boxers," she whispered again.

"Okay, well lift the covers and see, bitch," I said, waiting for her to do what I told her to do.

"Oh, my God!" she gasped.

I knew then that Dray was packing a monster. I was laughing hard as hell because the fear could be heard in her voice. My poor friend sounded like she was ready to run out of that damn room. I had to hold my stomach because I was laughing to the point I had to pee.

"Poe, his dick is big as fuck! Hell nawl, he ain't putting all that in me! That shit is gonna hurt," she said.

"Man the fuck up and stop acting like a baby, Kaymee. This is what the fuck you want. Ain't no reason to prolong this

134

shit. Ain't no better time than now. You will have to lose your virginity at some point and tonight is the night," I sang in my Betty Wright voice. "Besides, a lil' dick nigga is not what you want in a situation like this. You need a man that is gonna give you a night to remember."

She was quiet for a moment and I thought she hung up. I waited and just when I was about to say something, she agreed with me. "Okay, I'm about to get off this phone and get my nerves together to initiate this. I'll call you in the morning. Thanks, bestie. I owe you one. Pray for me."

She hung up before I could say anything else, looking down at the phone like, damn all right then. I placed the phone on the charger by the side of the bed and tried to go back to sleep. It was a no go because I was wide awake at that point. The good thing about it was I no longer had a headache.

I got up, slipped my feet into my slippers, and headed to the kitchen. My mama made a huge pan of lasagna and I didn't have an appetite earlier, but I was about to have a hefty plate as a midnight snack. Maybe that's what I needed to get that itis to go back to sleep.

Taking all of the Tupperware bowls out of the fridge, I put everything on the counter and got a plate out of the cabinet. The chunk of lasagna I cut was enough to feed two people. I had to think about what I was about to do and said fuck it. I scooped a spoonful of sweet peas and placed them on the plate. The garlic bread was in a glass bowl on the counter. I would nuke a couple pieces after my food was nice and hot.

About five minutes later, I was heading back to my room with my plate and a tall glass of Arizona Green tea with ginseng and honey. I was about to smash because I didn't realize how hungry I was until that moment. As I sat on my bed, the conversation that I had with Kaymee replayed in my head and I started laughing all over again. The good Lord knew I needed that laugh that night. It definitely cleansed my soul.

I turned the TV on after I turned the lamp on by the side of my bed. Waiting for my firestick to load, I thought about us leaving for Atlanta in a couple days. I was excited about going to school, but I couldn't wait to live the college life. The only thing I wasn't looking forward to was seeing Monty outside of Chicago.

Avoiding him had been easy in familiar territory, but it was going to be hard as hell until I learned my way around Atlanta. I picked up the remote and keyed in *All About the Benjamins*. I needed to laugh and take my mind off Mr. Watson. Eating and laughing at Reggie messing with Mr. Shelton at the store felt good for the moment.

*"I'm gon' start going to Dwight because you don't laugh at my jokes or nothing."*

*"Dwight, who?"*

*"Da white around yo' lip!"*

Mike Epps played the hell out of that part and when he started singing out those lottery numbers, I was singing right along with his crazy ass, damn near choking on the food that was in my mouth. I knew better than to try to eat and watch this movie.

Spooning the last of the lasagna into my mouth, my phone rang again. I didn't look to see who was calling because I knew it was Kaymee. It had been over an hour since I talked to her and I was ready for the tea.

"What, girl? You could've waited until later," I said, laughing into the phone.

"I'm far from a girl, but it's good to finally hear your voice."

Monty was the last person I expected to hear on my phone. I was kicking myself because I assumed and made an ass out of myself. Talking to him was not an option. There wasn't anything to discuss in my eyes. I sighed loudly into the phone. I was about to bang on his ass. He must've sensed it because he started talking fast as fuck.

"Poe, please don't hang up. Hear me out this last time, that's all I ask. You can hang up and never talk to me again if that's what you choose to do, but I need you to listen, baby," he pled into the phone.

"Don't call me baby, Montez. You lost that privilege when you stepped out on our relationship. Truthfully speaking, you said all that you didn't say at your house that day. I wasn't supposed to hear any of the things that were exposed from your damn cum guzzler!"

I had to calm myself down because my voice was no longer low and I didn't want my parents in my business. Getting upset was not an option either. I just got rid of the massive headache that I had been dealing with all damn day.

"She didn't mean anything to me, bae— I mean Poetry."

I had to stop his ass right there because two years of fucking with anyone means your ass was feeling something to keep returning. There was no way I was about to be persuaded otherwise. I loved him, but I refused to let love blind me. He could miss me with the bullshit because he had the right one.

"You mean to tell me sneaking back home without telling me you were here, inviting the bitch down to Atlanta, *and* keeping her ass a secret didn't mean shit to you," I hissed into the phone. He was quieter than a nigga that was standing on the corner miming for a living. "That was a muthafuckin' question, Montez! You wanted me to hear you out? Well, I'm doing that. But don't think for one second you weren't gonna listen to what the fuck I had to say, as well."

"I'm telling you that was only sex. I don't give a fuck about her! The only muthafucka I care about and love is you! Yeah, I fucked her for two years, but that's all it was. Nothing more, nothing less. I was wrong, Poe. The shit should've never happened and I'm sorry."

The tears fell from my eyes and I refused to let him know that I was crying. My heart was tightening up with every breath I took. I felt like I was having a damn heart attack. Letting this shit with him stress me out was not happening. I was too young to be going through this type of drama with a nigga.

Meesha

"I'm glad you actually know that you were wrong. You are a grown ass man that had the ability to understand your wrong-doings before it got that far. This shit hurts like hell. You wouldn't even know where to begin to try and even understand the level of pain I'm feeling. Love shouldn't hurt, Montez! I've been having trouble eating and sleeping over this bullshit! I'm going to eliminate myself from this equation. I can't forgive you for this. It's a level of hurt that I've never thought I would experience and I don't feel I can go on as if nothing happened."

At that point, I was crying a river and it was heard in every word I spoke. I really wasn't trying to lay my emotions on the table, but I couldn't help the way I felt. The pain in my stomach was intense. It was like I was hit with a blunt object.

"Please don't cry, Poetry. I feel like shit because you are crying because of me and there's nothing I can do to ease the pain. You are right. I could've walked away from Mena, but I didn't. All I want from you is a chance to make things right between us. I love you so much and I don't want to lose you. We have four years invested in this shit and I can't see myself not fighting for what we have."

"Make things right? You can't make something out of nothing! You don't realize that you lost me the minute your secret life was exposed. The shit would've continued had I not found out and don't say it wouldn't have because your ass would be lying through your teeth. For the record, we couldn't have invested four years into anything if you were fucking and sucking on a whole other person for two of those years! I'm not fighting for something that wasn't mine for the past two years. That shit is dead. I will be leaving in a couple days to go to Atlanta. Act like you don't know me when you see me in the streets."

I hung up the phone and turned it off. Knowing him like I did, my voicemail was going to be full and I would have plenty of text messages to go alone with it. I laid back on my pillow and cried until my eyes couldn't produce another tear.

138

## Chapter 16
### Jonathan

I had been out of the hospital for three days and I was feeling good enough to pay Dot's trifling ass a visit. Getting the address from Kaymee wasn't hard at all. I think deep down she wanted someone to kill the bitch, but that was too easy. Nah, she was going to suffer far worse than my daughter had. All the years of abuse she put her through was going to come back to her ten fold. She would be praying to God asking him to forgive her for all of her sins.

Approaching the entrance to the building Dot stayed in, I couldn't believe with all the money she was getting from me, she was still living in the projects. At least her mama got out of this hellhole with my child, even though she ended up right back in this muthafucka.

"Who you going to see, fam?" some lil' nigga had the nerve to ask me.

"It's none of your business who I'm going to see," I shot back.

"Nah, man. This my muthafuckin' building. If I don't know yo' ass, you can't go in."

Before that lil' nigga could blink good, he had a chrome .44 caliber at his dome. These punks needed to learn not to fuck with an OG. I've been where he was. My finger was resting on the trigger and I was ready to blow his stupid ass head off.

"He ain't worth it, Unc. Let that nigga go. He ain't on shit. You had one job and you almost lost your life trying to be hard. Whoever got yo' ass serving for them is stupid as hell. You're too fuckin' eager for altercations. Did you do what I paid you to do?" G walked up behind me out of nowhere.

"Yeah, G. I started giving her the laced twenties a couple weeks ago. At first, she held on to the three I gave her that night but once that monkey itch got to her ass, she's been back several times a day. She's a full-blown junkie now, big homie," he said, looking at me. "My bad, fam. I didn't mean anything about what went down. If I would've known that you were part of the Goon Squad, you would've been free to go in."

I laughed at his ass and shook my head. "With or without your permission, I was going in that building. If that meant all you niggas was gon' die, so be it. Respect yo' elders before you be walking around this bitch in spirit," I said, walking away from his ass with my gun still in my hand.

"I told yo' young ass to watch ya tongue. You gon' get ya'self killed, but thanks for handling that. That's Kaymee's daddy, by the way. He has every right to be here. Remember that for the future," G said to the lil stupid dude.

G walked up at the right time. I was on my way back to the joint. That kid was about to be on the news, real shit. There were too many dummies carrying guns thinking they were tough. When I up that thang, he was ready to shit is pants. His friends didn't move a muscle. They stood waiting for him to get his wig split.

We proceeded into the building and that muthafucka smelled like a dozen dead bodies were buried somewhere within the walls. I couldn't imagine having to live in the conditions that I was witnessing at that moment. There was garbage and condoms scattered around and don't let me start on the rodents. They had their own crew together running in packs, the shit was sad.

I didn't even want to wait for the elevator, so we took the stairs to the sixth floor. Being in the hospital and getting shot had a nigga out of shape like a muthafucka. As soon as I got the okay, I was going hard in the gym. The way I was breathing from climbing those stairs was something I wasn't used to.

G led the way to the apartment that Dot lived in. I wasn't about to touch shit in that bitch, so knocking on the door was something I wasn't going to do. He reached over and rapped on the door three hard times. We waited a couple minutes until I heard shuffling on the other side.

"Who the fuck is it?" she yelled out.

"Open the door, Dot," I said, while placing my piece behind my back.

She hesitated before unlocking the door. When she finally got the locks opened, I twisted the knob and pushed my way in. Dot didn't look like the woman I saw a couple weeks ago. Her eyes were sunken in, her hair was all over her head, and she was skinny as hell. I looked at her wondering how much shit had she been smoking in that small amount of time.

"Damn, you look fucked up, baby mama! I know damn well you ain't on that shit, are you?" I asked as G closed the door behind him.

She looked around nervously, trying to close her filthy housecoat. She was fidgeting as if something was about to jump out and attack her ass. I kind of felt sorry for her, but that went out the window when I thought about the shit she put my daughter through. That bitch named karma was in full effect.

"If you call smoking weed as being on that shit, then yeah. But don't try to make it seem like I'm a fuckin' crackhead, Jonathan! What are you doing at my house anyway? I've been living in this muthafucka for eighteen years and this is the first time you've stepped foot in here."

This bitch was trying to get smart at the mouth at the wrong damn time. She must've forgot that she shot me and my daughter and left us for dead. I could strangle her ass right now and throw her body down the garbage chute if I wanted to. She needed to slow her roll.

"The way you are looking around and clawing at your skin, weed ain't your drug of choice. A blind man can see that. I didn't know shit about your whereabouts until I got the address from my daughter. What the fuck was you thinking when you shot the gun that day, Dot? Do you know I could've died?" I asked, glaring at her with my fist balled up.

"Fuck you and that lil' bitch! My intentions were to kill the both of y'all, but I failed on both accounts. I wish like hell you had died. I was gunning for your bitch ass the hardest! You've been dead to me since the day you turned your back on me when I was pregnant, nigga."

I didn't care what she said about me, but calling my daughter anything other than the name she was given was disrespectful. Grabbing her by her throat, I squeezed just enough to cut off her air supply momentarily. She was struggling trying to loosen my grip, but she wasn't a match for me.

"If you ever disrespect my daughter in my presence again, I'll make sure you suck everything you eat through a straw for the rest of your life!" I gritted before I tossed her away from me. "You have traumatized her long enough and it ends now! From now on, the money that you have been getting from me is no more."

Her eyes grew big as hell when I said those words. The look of shock was replaced with an angry expression. "You owe me that money! I was the one that took care of *your* daughter her entire life! How do you expect me to pay my bills with no money, Jonathan?"

"Nah, you took care of yourself for the last twelve years. Your mother had Kaymee for the first six years of her life, that's how I got the chance to see her. You were never supposed to get those checks. You did a change of address after your mama died and didn't have the decency to contact me to let me know about it. If I had known, you knew the money train would have come to a halt. Your ass ain't a fool by a long shot, but your days of living off me are over. You will have to either get a job, or start charging niggas to suck their dicks from now on but that's not my problem. You are one lucky muthafucka because you could be floating in the river right now, but I'm gon' let you kill ya'self. Have a good life and tell Scotty I said hello."

I walked to the door and purposely left an ounce of laced weed on the table by the door. I didn't give a fuck if she smoked herself into a coma. The bitch was about to die slowly or she would be praying for the good Lord to send for her rotten ass.

"You muthafucka!" she screamed, charging at me.

She swung and tried to hit me in the face, but I threw my arm up in time to block it. Repeatedly throwing jab after jab, I finally reached in and grabbed her around the throat again. Her hits didn't hurt, but I wasn't going to let her think it was okay to hit me.

"When I let you go, I want you to keep your fucking hands to ya'self. It's taking everything in me not to murk yo' junkie ass right now," I said, tossing her a few steps back. "Get everything out now because it will be the last chance you will get to address this shit."

"You ruined my life before and now you are trying to do it again! I could've done so much with myself if you hadn't left me to be a single mother," she cried, while scratching her neck.

This bitch was geekin' and didn't even know it, the drugs were wearing off. She would need another hit real soon. I was laughing at what she said because I didn't do shit to her life, so I wasn't taking the blame.

"Your life is fucked up because of you, Dot. Not me, not Kaymee, and not your mama! Yo' ass! I will not be taking care of you anymore. My money will be used to take care of the daughter that I haven't seen in twelve damn years. You're on your own from this point on."

"I didn't finish school and I've never had a real job all because I had to take care of that lil' bi—girl! My life was put on hold so I could be a mother! What the fuck am I gonna do?" She started crying those fake ass tears she was forcing to come out of her eyes.

All I could do was shake my head. She was being extra as hell like I had a soft spot in my body and I would change my mind about what I said. Looking over at G, the vein in his forehead was protruding. He wanted to come over and kill her ass, but I told him no. Dot was going to see how it was to lose everything she had.

"Dot, you can stop all that shit. You had plenty of time to do whatever you wanted to do with your life. You made the decision to collect my tax-free dollars and live off welfare. It was your decision to choose partying over school. Your mother had my daughter for years. All you did was abused her and treated her like shit because you were mad at me. She had years of nothing living with you and that's a shame, Dot. You could've graduated high school, went to college, and started a career. Instead, you opted to be a hood chick and now you won't have a pot to piss in. It's your turn to see what it's like to have nothing," I said with my hand on the knob.

"What do you mean? You threatening me now?" she asked with a snarl on her face.

"Nah, it's a promise. Get ready to live a hard-knocked life, bitch. G, let's get the fuck outta here," I said, walking out the door.

## Chapter 17
### Kaymee

The night I gave my cookies to Dray was a night I would re-member for the rest of my life. My first time hurt like hell but started feeling good in a blink of an eye. After the first round, I couldn't get enough of him. I didn't want the way I was feel-ing to ever go away. I was taking his pipe like a grand cham-pion and he didn't complain one time.

It was Dray's decision to get some sleep after several hours of making love. I was pissed because I wanted to keep going. I learned many things in that time. Insisting on sucking his dick when I put it in my mouth, I gagged immediately because I had never had anything in my mouth other than edible shit.

*"You don't have to do it if you're not comfortable, bae,"* Dray said, trying to pull me up to lay next to him.

*"No, it's not that. I just have to get used to having it in my mouth. I want to get all the first of sex out of the way right now,"* I said with confidence, while looking up at him.

*He had this look of hope in his eyes and I didn't know what it was about. I was stroking his pipe gently, but his eyes never left mine and then the smirk appeared on his lips. Caressing the side of my face, his smile widened.*

*"So, do that mean you givin' up that ass, too?"*

*Confusion was displayed on my face because I knew damn well we had just spent countless hours fucking from here to Jerusalem. How the hell was he talking about if I was giving up the ass when he had me in every position imaginable? I sat up on my elbow and waited on him to explain what he was talking about.*

*"What the hell are you talking about, Drayton? You've been getting the ass since I opened my legs. I know damn well you didn't forget about what transpired after all that moaning and groaning you were doing,"* I said, laughing.

*"Nah, baby girl. I got a lot of that sweet shit between your legs. That shit was good, but I was talking about that dookie shoot between them plump cheeks," he said, licking his lips.*

*His ass was pushing his luck. He was lucky to get my kitty. I knew damn well he didn't think he was sticking all that dick in my ass. Shid, sometimes it hurt like a muthafucka to shit, so I knew his innuendo to fucking me in the ass was over the top. At that moment, I didn't even want to learn to give oral sex anymore. I was turned all the way off by that time.*

*Letting his dick fall from my hand, I rose up on my knees and crawled to the head of the bed, sliding under the covers. I pulled the covers over my shoulders and turned my back to him. "Don't ever bring that shit to me again. That sounds disgusting as hell. Stick to the gushy, because that hole will forever have a, 'do not enter sign on it'. I'm going to sleep, you should do the same," I said, closing my eyes.*

He wasn't mad that I went to sleep on him. The only thing he did was pulled me closer to him and held me throughout the rest of the morning. The feeling of being close to him was one I could get used to. What I couldn't get with was him trying to plunge in my backdoor. I was going to try to forget he brought that up though.

After we woke up, we hung out together the rest of the day and we had so much fun. He cooked for me and I ate every morsel. Dray was any woman's dream. The fact that he was my man was a bonus for me. Drayton Montgomery was my future and I couldn't wait to see what was in store for us.

The little things were what I enjoyed about him. He bought flowers, he made sure I had my favorite black walnut ice cream, and he actually loved me regardless of the things I've been through. I appreciate the fact that he always does things to keep me smiling. There's not a time that I'm sad when I'm around him. As long as he doesn't take part in Monty's shenanigans, he'd be good.

It was the day before we were set to leave for Atlanta and I was back at Mama Chris's house. Poetry and I had a day of fun planned to enjoy our city. It would be awhile before we would be able to come home for a visit, so we were going to have a ball. I knew for a fact I wanted a deep-dish pizza from Giordano's. I wasn't leaving Chicago without indulging in that pie. Garrett's was another spot I wanted to hit. The popcorn was off the chain and I needed that as a snack on the road.

Our first stop was Monty's house. Poetry wanted to get her things from his house that he never brought to her after the incident with Mena. The feeling I had in the pit of my stomach wasn't a good one. Something was telling me that things weren't going to go as smooth as I hoped.

"Poe, maybe I should call Dray and have him to bring your things here. Going to Monty's house don't feel like the right thing to do.

Poetry and I was in my room packing the remaining things for the move. It wasn't much, but I wasn't trying to leave anything behind. She glanced in my direction and rolled her eyes without responding to what I suggested.

"I guess that's a no to what I said, huh?"

"Monty and I talked and it's over between us. We don't hate one another and I don't need a middleman to handle my affairs, Kaymee. We are going over there so I can get my shit! It's either you're riding with me, or I'll go alone. Either way, I'm going," she said, tossing a shirt in my luggage.

Her mind was made up and there was no convincing her otherwise. We finished packing and she was ready to head out. I gathered my purse and my phone while searching for my itch stick. I had another week to deal with it and I couldn't wait for it to come off. It was hot, itchy, and irritating as hell.

"Shouldn't you call first, Poe?" I asked nervously.

"For what? I wouldn't have to go over there if he had brought my shit to me instead of poppin' up empty handed a million and three times! He will open the door and we will be in and out, let's go."

We left out the house and jumped in my truck heading in the direction of Monty's house. During the ride, the silence was driving me crazy, so I connected my phone to the Bluetooth. Ciara's new song, "Level Up", was what I selected and pressed play. When the beat dropped, both of us started bouncing in our seats.

"This is my new anthem! It's time for ya girl to level the fuck up, Mee!" Poe screamed.

She kept asking me to replay the track and I did whatever was needed to keep a smile on her face. The moment we hit Monty's block, I knew things were about to go from smiles to frowns. Monty was standing on the porch with an unknown female. He didn't seem too happy to see her but Poe didn't see it that way.

"Oh, I knew it was a reason I had to come over here," she said, whipping the truck into the driveway. Once she threw the gear in park, she reached for the door to get out but I hit the locks as she pulled the lever.

"Sis, don't' be on no bullshit. This is not what we came over here for. Who is that anyway?"

"That's Mena's bitch ass! But he ain't fuckin' with her no more. Yeah, okay. I'm not gon' say shit. I just want to get what's mine and be out," she said as the glass shattered out of the back-passenger window.

"Get the fuck out, bitch! I told you this wasn't over!"

That hoe had life all the way fucked up! Her beef was with Poe, but she damaged something that belonged to me. We jumped out of the truck at the same damn time and I got to her first because she was on my side of the car.

"Mee, hold on!" Monty yelled at me.

There was nothing to be said after she pulled that pussy shit. I ran up on her and clocked her ass in the middle of her forehead with my cast. She stumbled but I caught her by shirt before she fell to the ground. I couldn't allow her to go down that easily.

"I don't even know your stupid ass but you fuckin' up my shit!" I screamed as I plummeted her face.

Poetry came over and knocked me to the side, forcing me to let me go. "Nah, Mee. I got this. Square the fuck up, bitch. I don't believe in that two on one bullshit. You wanted me to get out, here I am."

Monty grabbed Poetry from behind trying to walk her away. What did he do that for? That gave Mena the opportunity to snake her in the face. Poetry struggled to get away from Monty but he wouldn't let her go. Mena moved in to swing again and I tried to knock her head into the middle of next week.

"Let her go, Monty! You see this bitch on that grimy shit!" I yelled at his ass.

Instead of letting Poetry go, he started hollering at Mena. "What the fuck is your problem, Mena? The shit you are doing is uncalled for! Go the fuck home!"

"I'm not leaving until I whoop this young bitch ass! Ain't shit you can do to stop me either. I'm not gonna do shit until you let her go!"

Poetry was battling to get out of the hold Monty had on her, but it wasn't working in her favor. "If you don't let me go now, I'm whoopin' yo' ass whenever you do. You allowed this hoe to hit me when you decided to restrain me. You should've been preventing her from throwing that damn brick, nigga! Let me go, Montez!"

"Y'all ain't about to be out here fighting, Poe. I don't give a fuck about the shit you talking,"

Wrong answer in my book. He didn't want to let her go so that only meant I had to take care of the lightweight. I punched her so hard I swear I heard her swallow her taste buds. "I know you didn't think an ass whoopin' wasn't coming because he is holding her, did you? Nah, it doesn't work like that."

"If you want to take this for ya girl, let's do it."

She charged at me and I knocked the wind out of her again with my cast by hitting her in her stomach. This bitch fucked up my truck and she hit my bestie when she couldn't defend herself. Yeah, she was about to get this work. I had pent up anger from all the shit I had been through and I was taking it out on her ass. She was bent over clutching her stomach, I used that moment to uppercut her under her chin. Her teeth clattered together loudly.

"Aaaaaaargh, you bitch!"

Monty let go of Poetry and ran over and grabbed me before I could stomp that bitch in the face. That's exactly what I wanted him to do because it gave Poetry the go ahead to smash her ass. He couldn't hold us both. Poetry grabbed Mena by the hair and punched her too many times to count in her face.

"I told you before that you were irrelevant to me. I don't give a fuck what's going on between y'all. Stay away from me!" Poe screamed with every punch she threw.

I thought Poe was going to break her damn neck the way her neck whipped back and forth. Poe wasn't playing with her. She was delivering straight Mike Tyson haymakers, hitting every target. Mena was leaking and I felt bad for her, but that didn't last long. Poe hit her one last time and she fell in a heap on the ground, knocking her out cold. I knew she was cool because her chest was moving up and down.

Monty let me go and grabbed Poe again as she moved toward Mena. "That's enough, Poetry! She's down, damn!" he yelled at her.

"Montez, get your hands off me! I told this bitch not to come for me unless I sent for her! This is your fault. Had you not given her the impression that I didn't matter, she wouldn't be lying in her own blood taking a nap. Now you can take her to the hospital and get her ass patched up. Remind this hoe that I'm not to be fucked with the next time my name comes out of her mouth!" she said, shrugging out of his grasp. "You are responsible for getting Mee's window fixed. We leave sometime tomorrow, so figure that shit out."

"I got that, don't worry about it. I'm sorry for all of this," he said lowly.

"Save that shit for somebody that's willing to listen. I'm not the one," she said, walking to the truck. "Come on, Kaymee."

Poetry got in the truck and started it up. I glanced at Monty and shook my head. Mena was lying on her back but she was moving slightly. I walked to the truck and opened the door. "Monty, you need to get this shit under control before someone gets seriously hurt. Talk to Mena and tell her to stay the fuck away from my friend. Don't worry about the window. I'll get it fixed myself. I don't like being in the middle of what's going on between y'all. I love both of you."

"Nah, here," he said, reaching in his pocket. Pulling out a knot of bills, he counted out five hundred dollars and tried to hand it to me.

I ignored his outstretched hand and got in the truck. When he saw that I wasn't going to take the money, he tossed it through the broken window and it landed on the floor as Poe backed out of the driveway.

"Poe, wait! I want to give him his money back."

"Kaymee, fuck him! We are about to go get your window fixed on his dime. He can kiss my ass! I'm so tired of this shit and it gives me another reason to walk away for good."

I didn't know where we were going to get the window fixed. I pulled my phone out and called my daddy. He would point me in the right direction.

"Hey, baby girl. How's it going?" he asked when he answered the phone.

"I need a recommendation to get my side passenger window fix."

"What happened, Kaymee? And don't lie."

I started explaining what happened, while wringing my fingers together. When I was done, he sent me a location of a shop and told me not to worry about paying. I entered the location into the GPS on my phone and it led us to the south side on 67$^{Th}$ and Ashland.

It took about twenty minutes to get there. Poetry parked
the truck and we went inside. My daddy was standing in the
lobby talking to a guy at the counter. I got happy every time I
talked to him because he was showing me that he was here to
stay. He dropped whatever he was doing to come to the shop.

"Daddy, I didn't know you were coming here," I said, hugging him.

"You thought I was gon' leave you out here by yourself?
Nah, I will always try my best to protect you at all costs. How
are you Poetry?" he said once he noticed Poe standing there.

"Hey, Jonathan. I'm good," she said, looking around the
lobby.

"Don't let a nigga have you out here fighting and shit. This
goes for both of y'all. That shit ain't worth the headache. If
you have to go through all of the drama, leave that shit alone,"
he said, staring at the both of us.

"That's a done deal. I'm not going through that anymore."

She walked away to the waiting area and started watching
TV. I knew she was hurt from seeing Mena at Monty's house
after what happened with them. Truthfully speaking, I think
Mena showed up without him knowing, but those were only
my thoughts. I didn't know the truth.

"Thank you, daddy, for everything," I said, kissing his
cheek.

"Anytime, baby girl. Don't ever hesitate to call me."

My phone rang, playing Monica's "Everything To Me". I
knew it was Dray without looking. Pulling it from my purse, I
answered and put the phone to my ear. "Hey, baby," I said with
a smile on my face.

"What the fuck is wrong with you, Kaymee? Yo' ass out
here fighting in these streets like a fuckin' hood rat! My
woman should know how to conduct herself as such. That was
not your battle to be fighting, so you had no business fighting
that girl. Next time, I'm gon' need you to let Poetry handle her
own shit! That was between them, not yo' gullible ass. Don't

make me have to say the shit to you again, man. You are trying to be something in life, act like it."

I didn't realize I had him on speaker. Trying to correct my wrong was a little too late. My daddy heard everything he said and he wasn't happy. The grimace on his face was one that said he was madder than a muthafucka.

"Give me the phone, Kaymee," he said with his hand held out.

"I got it, daddy. Allow me to handle this."

"Not today, baby girl. Give me the phone, now," he said a little too calmly.

The choice to handle the situation wasn't mine to make anymore. Handing him the phone, I knew things weren't about to go well for Dray. Jonathan cleared his throat before he placed the phone to his ear. The expression on his face told me Dray was still talking shit.

"The question to you is, what's your muthafuckin' problem, nigga? I'm gon' need you to mind ya tone when you're talking to my daughter. I don't repeat myself under any circumstances, but if I have to, shit ain't gon' end well for whomever is on the other side of my rant. See, Kaymee is mine. She belongs to me. You're just borrowing her. When you get tired of her, bring her back, or call me and I'll come get her. She bet not have a scratch on her either. Cuz if you put your hands on her, I will be fuckin' yo' punk ass up. Now, all that shit you were saying is something you may want to think about, patna. She is my prize possession now that I'm back in her life and I will give my life for her. I can't tell her who to be with, but you can best believe I'll be watching yo' ass from this point on."

I couldn't believe my daddy chopped his ass up the way he did. It was my fault he heard what was said to begin with. I was curious to know what else Dray said to piss Jonathan off like that. Before he gave my phone back, he was about to say something but walked away instead. I was worried about how Dray was feeling about what my daddy said to him.

"Umm, hello," I whispered into the phone.

"The shit you just did was foul, Kaymee. You put the phone on speaker purposely," his voice boomed in my ear.

"I didn't. It was an accident. What the hell were you saying, Dray?"

"It doesn't even matter. I'll holla at you later," he said, hanging up on me.

Calling his phone back to back, he never picked up. We had been going strong without any problems. Now he was ignoring me like a stranger. I was going to give him time to cool off, but on the inside I wanted to cry a river. Hopefully, he would come around at some point.

Jonathan walked from the back and over to where I was still standing, trying to get Dray back on the phone. I instantly got nervous and scared at the same time. My mind went back to when Dot was upset with me. It always ended with me getting hurt.

"Baby girl, let's go outside and talk. Your truck will be ready in fifteen minutes. That would give me enough time to say what I have to say."

I didn't realize my truck was being worked on. I never gave them my keys. Poetry still had them in the waiting room with her. Nodding my head, I led the way to the door. When we got outside, Jonathan didn't waste any time getting to the point. My nerves were on an all-time high and I didn't know how to get them under control.

"Kaymee, I didn't appreciate how that nigga was talking to you when he called. Don't ever let a muthafucka speak to you in that manner. Once you start letting him treat you like shit, he will continue to do so. I don't give a fuck what you did. You only got one daddy and that's me."

"He didn't mean anything by what he said. He is pissed because I was fighting with Poetry and Mena—"

"That don't give his ass the right to raise his fuckin' voice at you! I can't tell you who to deal with relationship wise, but you will not allow him to disrespect you. I will be here for you

154

whenever you need me. You better call me if that nigga *ever* thinks about putting his hands on you and I mean that shit."

The words my daddy said to me hit hard. I didn't believe Dray would put his hands on me, nor did I think he would do me wrong. I was going to wait until he calmed down before I tried to apologize.

"Thanks for looking out for me. Dot would've said something negative about the situation. I want you to know that Dray is not that type of man. He won't hurt me," I said with confidence.

"Listen to me, any man is capable of hurting a woman, including myself. It may not be intentionally, but it can be done. You haven't known him long at all, so take things slow. With you defending him like you are, that tells me that you love him. I'm gon' school you real quick about men, baby girl. In the beginning, everything always seems sweets as candy. Keep your eyes open for the changes that are bound to surface when you get on his territory. He doesn't have anyone but you here in Chicago, but you will be with him in Atlanta and the real him will surface. I may be wrong, he could be a stand-up guy, but time will tell. Come to me about questions you may have, you have already walked into this relationship blindly. I believe I'm gon' have to fuck him up, truthfully speaking. Come on, your car should be ready."

We walked back inside and sure enough, the window to my car was fixed. I looked inside the waiting area and Poetry was watching *The Maury Show*. There was a woman that had been on the show six times and still hadn't found out who the father of her son was. It was sad as hell, but Poe loved that shit.

"Poe the car is finished, let's go. I'm hungry as hell and some stuffed pizza sounds good right about now," I said as I stood next to her.

"Hold on, Mee. I gotta see how this shit gon' end."

She was laughing at the woman that was a thousand percent sure the dude sitting on the stage was the father. Maury pulled out the results and read what was on the card.

*"In the case of two-year-old, Trevon. Devin, you are not the father!"*
Tiffany ran her ass off the stage and flopped on the floor. She was kicking and screaming as if she didn't know what the results would reveal already.

Poetry had tears running down her face from laughing so hard. "Her ass knew that baby wasn't his! That man didn't have anything to do with producing that baby. I don't know why these females go on this show to embarrass themselves."

She stood up, putting her purse over her shoulder. As I looked up, my truck was being pulled out to the front of the shop. I walked out of the door and my daddy was shooting the shit with a young cat. "Daddy, I'm about to get out of here. Thanks, again. We're about to go to Giordano's. You want to join us?"

"Nah, I have some things to take care of before we leave. I'll be through to get y'all about six in the morning. I need y'all to be ready, okay?"

"We'll be ready, I promise. I'll text you Poetry's address. That's where we'll be," I said, climbing in the truck.

"A'ight, baby girl. Remember what we talked about. Tell that nigga he don't want no smoke. Drive safely, Poetry and y'all be careful," he said, stepping back on the curb.

"Okay, daddy," I whined.

When we pulled off, I googled the southside Giordano's location. I told Poe to keep heading north on Ashland until she got to 55th street, then she made a right when we got there and headed east toward Hyde Park. We had to park damn near a block away because parking was scarce in that area. Surprisingly, we didn't have to wait to be seated.

Once we were seated, Poe grabbed a menu. I knew exactly what I wanted before I even got there. I stopped eating pork a while ago, so a good ole veggie pizza was calling my name. The waitress came right over to take our order.

"Good evening, are you guys ready to order or do you need a couple minutes?"

"No, I would like a medium super veggie deep dish, please. I would like a pink lemonade without ice."

"I guess we will be ordering two damn pizzas then. I'm far from a rabbit," Poetry said.

The waitress couldn't help laughing because the way she said it was hilarious. She hated when I ordered pizza because I always had to have spinach, green peppers, mushrooms, onions, broccoli, and black olives on it. She always stated how much she needed meat in her life.

"I'll have the meat and more meat deep dish, but can you hold the salami and add more sausage?" she asked the waitress.

"Sure, I can. What would you like to drink with that?"

"I'll take a Pepsi, please," Poe said, handing the menus to her.

As we waited for our food to arrive, I told her what happened while we were at the shop. She wasn't too pleased with the tone Dray used or the things that he said to me. "I wish I would've known about that shit while he was saying all of that, I would have cussed his ass out, too. He didn't come off as a nigga with a bad temper. As a matter fact, he has been very kind and loving to you. I can understand him being upset about you fighting, but why get hostile to the point that Jonathan had to put his ass in his place?"

"Truthfully speaking, I don't know why he came at me like that. He didn't give me the chance to explain when my daddy gave me the phone back. When I called him back after he hung up on me, he didn't answer. I'll try to call him back later."

Poetry stared at me with a look that screamed, "I wish you would". "You will not call his ignorant ass! Let him call you since he wanted to act like a jackass. He's been around that nigga Monty too muthafuckin' long. He will mess around and get his feelings hurt. You gave him the cookies and now he thinks he owns you. Don't let him get away with that shit or he will walk all over your ass, Mee."

She sounded like Jonathan and I couldn't be mad at either one of them because they were just looking out for me. Dray was wrong and I will call him out on his shit. The feedback I got, the more apologizing was something that wasn't going to happen. I would see if he would explain himself and he would have to apologize to me.

"Poe, I have to call him to ask what all of that was about. I won't apologize, but I don't want to go to Atlanta and we're on bad terms."

Smacking her lips, she rolled her eyes and glanced away from me. The waitress came over with our pizzas. My mouth watered instantly and the subject was forgotten for the moment. I ate my first slice as if I hadn't eaten in a week and I reached for a second helping. The sound of a text came through on my phone. I wiped my hands on a napkin and pulled it from my purse.

My first thought was it was Dray, but when I looked at the screen, Dot's name was displayed. I was very reluctant to even open the message. I hadn't heard from her since the day she tried to kill me. Trying to figure out what she could possibly have to say to me, I followed my first mind and ignored the text. I placed the phone on the table and started eating again.

"Who are you over there ignoring, Mee? I hope it's Dray's ass," Poe said with a mouthful of pizza.

"No, it wasn't him. It was Dot actually. I don't have anything to say to her."

Cutting a piece of pizza, I placed it in my mouth and savored the herbs as my eyes closed. The flavor was dancing in mouth. The sound of my phone going off again interrupted my taste bud orgasm. I picked the phone up because my curiosity was at an all-time high. I opened the text and I couldn't believe what I was reading.

**Dot: Bitch, I wish I had killed yo' ass! You gave Jonathan my address so he could come to my house and threaten me! Bitch, you are going to regret that shit!**

**Dot: Oh, you don't have to respond. Believe me when I tell you, your life is about to be hell! If you think you will**

**leave and succeed in Atlanta, think again, bitch. We will be miserable together. Just wait and see!**

Yes, I gave my daddy the address because he asked for it, but I didn't have anything to do with whatever happened when he went there. Why didn't she take that up with him? She was out of her mind if she thought her tactics were about to intimidate me. I was ready for whatever she had planned for me. I was done trying to respect her because she was my mother. All of that went out the window when she shot me.

Pressing the box at the bottom of the screen, my fingers were going a mile a minute. This was the last time I was going to entertain her bullshit. My life was on the path to greatness and Dot Morrison didn't have a slot in it.

**Me: If your life is miserable, that's all on you. Don't blame me for your mishaps. I cried out for years for your love and affection and you gave zero fucks. Now that I'm doing a you on your ass, you have a problem with it. I'm going to continue to level up and I want you to see my progress and keep hating like I know you are. There is nothing that's going to prevent me from succeeding and that includes you. Stay out of my life, Dot, because you won't get the opportunity to bring me down. I've already surpassed the point you are trying to make it to. Have a nice life, mother. I plan to do just that! Remember one thing, God don't like ugly, so choose your battles wisely.**

I closed out the message and put my phone back on the table and Poetry was staring at me intensely. "What was that about?"

"The same typical Dot bs that I will no longer dwell on. She's with the shits with her threats that are not moving me the way it used to. She'll be okay, though. I'm ready to go. Where to next?" I asked, finishing the slice that was in front of me.

"Don't get mad at me. I know we had plans for the day, but I'm tired. After working that hoe over earlier, I just want to go home and relax. My head has been hurting for hour. I thought I just needed to eat, but it's still throbbing."

Why didn't you say that earlier? We could've gotten the pizza to go. I'm tired too, so we can go back to the house and relax. Jonathan will be at the house bright and early, so we can head out. I'm too excited about starting a new life."

"Girl, you and me both. It's about to be epic in ATL. I can't wait," Poetry said, waving the waitress down.

We paid the bill and boxed up the remaining slices that I knew were going to get maxed later. The minute I was settled in the passenger seat, I felt as if I would pass out. The day was filled with bullshit that hopefully would come to an end once we left the Windy City.

Love Shouldn't Hurt 2

## Chapter 18
### Montez

I was in the crib chillin' watching *Menace to Society* while having a drink. The conversation I had with Poetry was one that was still on my mind. I had truly hurt her with the things I did. There was nothing else to do except wait and see if she would find her way back to me. She was right, I brought all of this on myself.

Mena had been blowing my line up, but I hadn't answered once and didn't have any intentions of doing so. I had her on the block list, but she would call from someone else's phone. I still didn't answer because if I didn't know the number, I wasn't fucking with it. All the texts that she sent were erased without being read. I was serious when I said I was done with her.

I decided earlier that we would get a head start on the road back down south. There wasn't any reason to hang around the Chi anymore. The doorbell rang and I wasn't thinking about answering it because whoever was on the other side should've phoned first. I continued watching Caine get interrogated at the police station and the shit made me laugh every time.

The doorbell was being rung repeatedly over and over and it was starting to piss me off. I stormed to the door and yanked it open, Mena was standing there looking pitiful as hell. I didn't know what she was there for, I said everything I needed to say to her weeks ago.

"What's up, Mena?" I asked, leaning against the door-frame.

"I just wanted to see you before you left, Montez. I've missed you so much. Why have you been ignoring my calls? I thought we were better than this."

"To be truthful, I don't have anything to say to you. We discussed if we had to part ways and you were on board with the things that were said. You do remember saying there wouldn't be any problems if it came to that, correct?"

161

She stood looking at me without answering, so I continued. "Mena, you knew I had a woman. All you were to me was a piece of pussy, there's a difference. You were convenient when my girl couldn't come out. I warned you not to catch feelings."

"Hold the fuck up! You were sucking and fucking me like I was your bitch, but you want me to keep my feelings in check? How was that supposed to happen when you came to my house making love to me? We didn't fuck once, Montez. You took your muthafuckin' time and stayed days at a time. When you fuck somebody, you don't cuddle afterwards. A fuck buddy don't get all expense paid trips to Atlanta, Atlantic City, or Vegas. You are pissed at me because your shit came out for your girl to see. You enjoyed having two women whenever you wanted, admit the shit," she cried.

Her points were valid, but I had to do what needed to be done in order to enjoy the time I gave her. It still didn't make it more than what it was. I was going to those places anyway but I invited her along because she was of age to go with me. Poetry wasn't old enough to gamble, so why not have my side-piece with me?

"I didn't enjoy having two women because I only had one. What part of you were nothing to me don't you understand? I didn't have to beg you to suck my dick or fuck me, Mena. You assumed the position from day one, ma. As long as you were opening up to me, I was diving in. Yeah, I feasted on your goods, and you enjoyed that shit, too. I knew you were devoted to me and wasn't fucking with no other niggas. Why not go the whole nine yards to please you? All you had to do was play your position, but you had to run ya mouth like that would force me to choose you. How did that work out for you?" I said and smirked.

"You are only acting this way because you think your girl coming back to you. She's not, but I'm the one that's willing to put all of this behind us and love you the long way. So, how about you let me in so I can make you smile? The frown on your face is not sexy at all," she said, licking her lips while running her hand down my chest.

"Nah, that's not happening. Get away from my house and don't come back, Mena," I said knocking her hands off me and pushing her back slightly.

Waiting for her to go back to her car, I saw a truck whip into my driveway and I got lost in Poetry's eyes. She was trying to get out of the truck but Mee was saying something to her. When she looked up, all I saw was fire in her expression. I was so focused on Poetry, that I didn't see Mena pick up one of the decorative bricks in my front yard and hurled it into the back window of Mee's truck.

"Get the fuck out, bitch! I told you this wasn't over!"

I rushed down the steps because both Poe and Mee jumped out at the same damn time. Mee rocked Mena with her cast and started punching her over and over. She was on her ass like bees to honey and I thought she was going to kill her. Poe pushed her out of the way and started screaming for Mena to go toe to toe with her.

I grabbed Poe because they weren't about to fight. I fucked up by doing that because Mena ran up and sucker punched Poe. Mee was screaming for me to let her go when Mena tried to get another hit in. She didn't make it because Mee rocked her ass, but Mena was still talking shit. Mee used that damn cast again and I didn't have any choice except to let Poe go to grab her.

Keeping both of them off Mena was impossible. Poe got hold of her and fucked her up. Mena was laid out on the ground. Poe snapped on me and jumped in the truck. I threw money for the damage in the window when Mee wouldn't take it as they drove off. Watching them speed down the street until I couldn't see the truck anymore, I turned to check on Mena.

"Come on so I can get you to the hospital. Why the fuck would you throw a brick through her shit, Mena?" I asked as I helped her up.

She pushed me in my chest and stepped in my face. "Fuck you, Montez! I told her that shit from a few weeks ago wasn't over! I don't need to go to the hospital, I'm outta here and you don't have to worry about me anymore."

"Mena, you sound stupid as hell. You got your ass beat then and you just got fucked up today. Was it worth it? Nah, it wasn't and I told you before you brought ya ass over here that I was done with your ass! Don't act like you're doing me a muthafuckin' favor. I've been told you we were done."

She wiped her mouth with the back of her hand and walked to her car. Once she was settled in the driver's seat, she let her window down and stared at me evilly. "Montez, I loved you with all of my heart but I was a game to you. I hope whoever you get with next, dogs your yellow ass out! You don't deserve to be happy you bastard! Your daddy should've sucked the cum out his own dick instead of producing your dirty ass!"

I stormed toward her car and she quickly threw it in gear and peeled out of my driveway. The only thing I wanted was for her to leave and she did that. As I walked back to the house, I started laughing hard as hell because the last crack she threw at me was funny as fuck. Mena was big mad and all because I cut her ass off the pipe.

When I entered the house, Dray's black ass was coming out of the guest room scratching his balls. His ass was ashy as fuck looking dead and shit. I knew he didn't sleep through all that damn noise that was going on outside, his scary ass was probably waiting until it was over.

"Nigga, I know you wasn't sleep through all that noise."

He stopped in the hallway with a perplexed expression on his face. "What the fuck are you talking about, fam?"

"You were seriously sleeping while I was struggling to be a referee around this muthafucka, huh?"

"Would you just tell me what went on without all the stupid questions? Hell yeah, I was sleeping. You were the one that want to leave at nightfall to hit the highway. I needed to sleep so I can drive first, nigga."

"Mena brought her ass over here trying to question a nigga about why I wasn't answering her calls. As I'm trying to get her away from my spot, Poe and Mee pulls up and Mena's stupid ass threw a brick through the window. Mee beat her ass while I was holding Poe. When I let Poe go to get Mee, Poe went in on her ass. The shit was wild and I think I've lost Poe for good now. I know she thinks I'm still fucking with Mena's ass."

He didn't reply to what I said. He only made a beeline back to the room and slammed the door. A couple minutes passed before I heard his voice boom through the door. He was yelling at someone but I couldn't make out what was being said. Then he got quiet for a while and there wasn't any talking after that. He walked out of the room looking like the Incredible Hulk heading for the bathroom.

I waited until he came out to see what was going on. He walked to the kitchen without saying anything until he grabbed a bottled water out of the fridge. "Man, Monty. Jonathan is gon' make a nigga smack his ass. He needs to stay the fuck out of my relationship with Mee."

"What the fuck happened?" I was lost because I didn't know what happened that damn fast.

"I called Kaymee's ass and asked her what the fuck was she thinking out in the streets fighting. Ain't no woman of mine gon' be acting like no damn hood rat. Her ass had the fuckin' phone on speaker and Jonathan heard me going off on her. He talking about she only got one damn daddy! What the fuck, nigga! I'm her muthafuckin' daddy behind closed doors! I hung up on her ass and turned the ringer off. I think she did that shit on purpose," he said, drinking from the water bottle.

"Mee is not that type of female, Dray. Jonathan is right. She only has one daddy. Shid, you can't blame him for speaking his mind if you were hollering at his daughter, fam. He had every right to say something. I think you owe her an apology because that fight was brought to them. Mena started that shit. Had you let me finish the story, you would've known that."

I wasn't about to let him blame her for the shit that happened out there. That wasn't even Mee's fight, but her and Poe were riding for each other for life. She had every right to whoop Mena's ass for fuckin' up her ride, too.

"Damn, well I'll apologize but it won't be over the phone. I'll do that shit when she touches down in Atlanta. What time are we leaving?" he asked, heading back down the hall.

I looked at my watch and it was a little after seven in the evening. "We can leave at about midnight, if that's cool with you."

"Yeah, that's cool. We took the rental back the other day. There's nothing else to do, but I'm going back to sleep. Wake me up at eleven so I can get ready, nigga," he said, closing the door to his room.

I walked to the fridge, grabbed a Corona, and went to my room to roll a fat one before hitting the pillow to snooze. The day's events had my body feeling like I had lifted four hundred pounds of steel.

## Chapter 19
### Poetry

"Poe, it's time to get up. Jonathan will be here in a couple hours and we need to make sure we have everything that we're taking with us by the door."

Kaymee was about to get karate chopped in her throat if she didn't leave me the fuck alone. It wasn't going to take no time to get all of our stuff to the door. Majority of the shit was in boxes anyway. She was just excited to be getting the fuck away from Dot's crazy ass. I wanted to sleep until five thirty.

"Mee, leave me the hell alone, please. What time is it anyway? You better not say three o'clock either."

"It's not three, it's four," she said, laughing.

I didn't see shit funny because I wasn't getting up. "Get out right now, asshole. I knew I should've kept you up last night. You had too much damn sleep, in this muthafucka acting like the energizer bunny," I said, turning back over in the bed.

She had the nerve to turn my light on and I was livid. I jumped up and pushed her ass toward the door. "Don't bring your ass back until the sun start peeking out the fuckin' clouds! The roosters ain't even up at this time of the morning with yo' playful ass!"

"Poetry Renee, you must be out of your damn mind cussing in my damn house like that!"

I really wanted to beat Mee's ass now. If her ass would've left like I told her to, my mama wouldn't't have caught me cussing. Big booty was standing in the corner laughing and shit, but I had something for her ass.

"My bad, ma, but would you tell her to get out of my room? It's too early to be up, man."

"It's not too early when it takes you two hours to get yourself ready. Are you all packed and ready to go? I think all of y'all things should be at the door when Kaymee's dad gets here."

"Told you, Poe," Mee said, standing behind my mom.

I didn't have anything nice to say to her at that moment, so I kept my mouth closed. I had plans to fuck her up as soon as I got the chance. She was in this bitch acting like a five-year-old and shit, then she was making faces. She was the irritating sister I never had growing up, stankin' ass heifa.

"Hush ya face, Mee, before you get slapped," I shot back at her. "I have all of my things together, ma. All I need to do is put everything by the door. Can I go back to sleep, please? I'm tired. Mee can move my stuff since she got sleep last night and I didn't."

"I shouldn't do nothing for you since you wanted to be mean. You're lucky I love you. Now go back to bed, jerk."

"Enough of the name calling, Kaymee. Get out before I go get my belt and whoop both of you."

Kaymee looked at me and we both started laughing hard as hell. My mama didn't think it was funny and brushed passed Mee and went down the hall. We were still laughing when she came back swinging the belt. Kaymee ran to the bed and jumped under the covers with me. She was fucking us up with that belt.

"Okay, ma. We're sorry. Daddy!" I screamed when she wouldn't stop swinging the belt at us.

"What the fuck is he going to do? I told y'all asses to cut it out."

"Chris, leave my babies alone! It's three thirty in the damn morning and you're up acting a damn fool," he said, attempting to take the belt from her. She started hitting him on his legs. The way he was jumping around had me damn near on the floor. They looked so cute.

"Okay, Chris. That's it," he said, scooping her up. He threw her over his shoulder and started walking out of the room. "Don't leave my house until y'all give me some suga to go. I have to go put ya mama to bed real quick."

"Ewwwww, daddy! That's nasty!" I shouted after him. I heard him laughing as he made his way down the hall.

168

I wasn't even sleepy anymore because of these mutha-fuckas, so I got up and started getting my things together. Kay-mee helped me take my boxes and bags to the door and we did the same with her things. By the time we finished, it was five o'clock. That gave us enough time to shower and get dressed.

We were sitting in my room when Mee's phone rang and it was Jonathan. She put the phone on speaker when she answered. "Hey, daddy. Are you on your way?" she asked.

"I just dropped the car off at Enterprise and G is bringing me there. The problem is you never texted me the address."

"I thought I did that yesterday at the shop. I'll send it now. My bad."

"Are you girls ready to hit the road?"

"Yes, we're ready. We have everything by the door wait-ing for you to put in the truck."

"Waiting for me? What I look like, your maid?" he asked, laughing.

"Noooooo, you're my daddy! Some of those boxes are heavy."

"We can put the stuff in the truck, Jonathan," Poetry said into the phone.

"That's okay, Poetry. Thanks anyway. At least one of you is willing to help. I'll be there in about twenty minutes"

"Okay, we'll be ready. See you soon," she said, ending the call.

I went in the kitchen and heated up a couple slices of pizza for Mee and me. The rest would have to stay here with my parents. It was too early for this shit, but I was hungry as hell. Walking back into my room, I handed Mee her plate and sat on the bed. She was texting on her phone with a puzzled look on her face.

"What's wrong with you?" I asked, putting a chunk of pizza in my mouth.

"I've texted Dray so many times since last night and he hasn't texted back. He hasn't even looked at the messages. I don't know what to do now. Thanks for the pizza. I'm starving."

"What you need to do is let his ass contact you. He owes you an apology, not the other way around. You didn't do anything wrong."

She was quiet as she ate. I had to remember she was not as strong as I am and this is her first relationship. So, I kind of understood why she was trying so hard to get in touch with him. Unfortunately, I'm the one that's not in the profession to chase a nigga that don't want to be caught. I'll just be here for her whenever she needs me.

Her phone rang and she answered, getting up walking out of the room. I finished the last of my pizza and grabbed the plates to take them to the kitchen. Mee was at the door and I heard voices outside. I knew then that Jonathan was there to pick us up. Rinsing the plates and the utensils, I placed them into the dishwasher.

I walked to my parent's bedroom and knocked on the door. "Come in," my dad called out.

My dad was lying in the bed with my mom snuggled under him. They looked so in love and I couldn't stop the smile that displayed on my face. The type of love that my parents had for each other was one that I wanted for myself. You don't see many marriages lasting twenty years today.

"Jonathan is here to pick us up and I wanted to let y'all know that I will be leaving as soon as the truck is packed."

"Okay, baby. I'll wake your mom and we will be out shortly," he said, sitting up on his elbow. "Poetry, I want you to know that I'm very proud of you and Kaymee. I want you girls to go to Atlanta and kick ass academically. Have fun too, but responsibly. Conduct yourself as if your mom and I are still there with you. Use what we instilled in you to make the proper choices. I know you are going to continue to make us proud because that's the way I raised you. I'm going to miss having you around the house, but I've come to the realization that my baby is no longer a baby. I love you, Poe," he said with tears in his eyes.

Entering the room completely, I walked to the side of the bed my dad was on and hugged him tightly. The tears that welled in my eyes fell down my face. I was scared of leaving the protection of my parents, but I needed to make a life for myself. I wouldn't disappoint them. I would do all I could to succeed.

"I love you, too, daddy," I sobbed as I let him go after kissing his cheek.

"We will be out as soon as we get dressed."

Nodding my head okay, I left out of the room and closed the door.

Jonathan, Katrina, and G were standing in the living room with Kaymee when I entered. G had her in a headlock and she was laughing trying to get out of his grip. The scene before me dried the tears in my eyes because my friend was finally happy. It took a long time for God to bring her family to her and she deserved it.

"G, you are going to have to let my bestie go or we are both about to beat your body," I said getting in a boxer's stance.

"Poetry, you don't want those kinds of problems. I was only supposed to drop this fool off. Now I have to do manual labor by packing up this truck. The sun ain't even up and I have to work without pay."

"That's what family do," I said, laughing. "Hey, Jonathan and Katrina."

I walked over and gave both of them a hug before I slapped G upside his head, forcing him to let my friend go. He laughed and stepped back, rubbing his head as he glared at me wickedly.

"I'm gon' let you have that only because you a girl. Grab a box or something and take it to the truck."

"Nope, that's why you are here. Get to work, playa," I said, laughing at him.

"Come on, nephew. Let's start packing this shit up because I want to hit the road as soon as possible," Jonathan said, kissing Katrina on the cheek.

While they packed the truck, Kaymee, Katrina, and I sat at the kitchen table talking. We were laughing and thinking of things we wanted to do once we hit college grounds. Everything was going well until Katrina mentioned Monty.

"What did you decide to do about your relationship with Montez, Poetry? I hope you took my advice and talked to him. The last thing you want is drama interfering with your schooling."

"I sure did and there will be no kind of drama. Ending the relationship was the best decision to make. I still love him, but I don't think I will be able to forgive him for what he did. I'd rather let it go than be miserable any day."

"I totally understand and that shows maturity in you. Many young girls like the drama behind a man. I'm glad you're not one of them," she said, turning to Mee with a solemn expression. "You, young lady. I know we just met but your dad talked to me about the interaction he had with Dray. He wanted to kill that boy for the way he raised his voice at you. All I have to say about that is once you allow a man to disrespect you, he will think it's okay to continue."

"But he didn't disrespect—"

She cut her off before she could finish what she was about to say. "Kaymee, when a man raises his voice at you in the manner that he did, it's a form of control. I know there wasn't anyone around to teach you about love and relationships, but I want you to know that I'm here for you. Don't think twice about coming to me about anything, okay?"

I had to say what was on my mind. My bestie wasn't seeing the picture Katrina was laying before her. "Mee, Dray disrespected you, boo. You can't let him talk to you like you ain't nothing. He bet not ever let me hear him talking to you like that."

Dray was going to get out of his body again. It was the matter of when it would take place. My parents walked into the room looking sad. The hard part of going away for school was going to be leaving them. This would be the first time I'd be away from home for a long period of time.

"Hey, you guys. Are you all packed and ready to go?" my dad asked.

"Jonathan and G are putting everything in the truck now. Mom, dad, this is Katrina, Jonathan's girlfriend. Katrina, my parents, Chris and Stan," I said, making the introductions.

"Nice to meet you, Katrina. I'm so happy there will be a woman to look after my girls. I haven't had the privilege of meeting her dad, but please make sure they stay out of trouble. These two young ladies have never been a problem, so I'm not too worried. It's the fact of them going out into the real world that bothers me."

"The pleasure is all mine," Katrina said, standing up to shake their hands. "They will be great on their own. They are very respectable and still have a lot to learn about life. I will look out for them but they will have to live their life for them. Jonathan and G should be coming back in for another load soon, I'm quite sure he would be pleased to meet you."

They walked in at that precise moment, all heads turned toward the door when they entered. A smile appeared on Kaymee's face when she saw Jonathan. The happiness that he brought to her life was everything to me.

"I may have to get a moving truck for all this stuff y'all are taking on this move," Jonathan laughed. "Oh, I'm sorry. I'm Jonathan and this is my nephew Grant," he said, walking over to my parents.

"Nice to meet you and hello, Grant. Good to see you again. Jonathan I'm glad you are doing better. It was a shame what happened to you and Kaymee. You came into her life at the right time, she needs you. I did my part the last couple of years, but it wasn't enough. There's nothing like a parent's love," my mom spoke from her heart.

Meesha

"Mama Chris, I appreciate all that you've done for me. I could never repay you, but I love you so much. Stepping in when I had nobody else was all I needed," Kaymee said with tears in her eyes. "I'm going to miss you guys, but we'll be back to get on y'all nerves," she said, hugging my parents.

"We love you too, Kaymee," my dad said into her hair.

"Thank you for looking out for her. That was Dot's job and she failed miserably. I can't make up for the time I've lost, but I will try my best to be the best father that I can be to her now. She is my focal point and I will make sure that the both of them are taken care of in my neck of the woods. It was nice meeting you both, but I have to finish packing for the Queens of Chicago."

"Thanks for that, man. I will help you guys. They are my daughter's, too. Plus, I can't wait to turn their rooms into a gym and an office," my dad said, laughing as he headed for the door.

"You wouldn't!" I yelled to his back.

He glanced over his shoulder with a smirk, "But I am." He winked as he picked up four boxes.

The three of them gathered up the last of the load and went out of the door. Reality kicked in. I was really leaving to attend college. Nervousness took over my body and I had to shake it off. When I got anxious or upset, my head started to hurt. I didn't want to deal with that on the road.

My mom gathered both of us in her arms and held us tightly. "I want you all to go to Spelman and dominate with the knowledge that's within. You are leaving Chicago as young ladies, but will return as successful grown women. I have faith that the two of you will do great." Releasing us, she stepped back and grabbed my hands, looking me in the eyes. "Poetry, I can see the nervousness in your face, baby. I am a phone call away, no matter what time. You know I will be on the first thing smoking if need be."

The words my mom spoke were all true and I got emotional. Tears streamed down my face as she gathered me in her

174

arms. They were tears of joy and fear wrapped in one. At first, I was comfortable about going to school because Monty would be with me. Now, it was only going to be Mee and me. I soaked my mom's shirt with tears and snot and she didn't mind. Laying my head on her shoulder, I was trying to get myself together when Mee started to speak.

"Mama Chris, we will look out for each other. You don't have to worry. You already know we are about to go down south and kick butt. We will both come back ready to check a bag or two in the medical field. Future nurses on deck," Kaymee said, smiling.

The door opened and the men walked in looking exhausted. They were doing too much, acting as if they had just loaded an entire house of furniture on a moving truck. "Okay, ladies. Everything is packed and ready to go. It's time to hit the road," Jonathan said.

Kaymee and I gathered our purses and made sure we had our phones, chargers, and ear buds for the ride. Hugging my parents one more time and letting them know that I would call along the way, we left out and piled in the truck.

\* \* \*

Katrina had a cooler filled with water and juice along with sandwiches and snacks for us to eat on the ride to Atlanta. We started off singing and laughing and before I knew it, Kaymee was knocked out. We had been driving four hours and I was wide awake. I decided to read *"Falling for A Hitta"* by Krystal Armstead. Her pen has never disappointed me. The story started with suspense and I wanted to know what happened. I couldn't stop reading even though my eyes were tired. Easy was my kind of dude. He was a white boy with swag and I loved it! He didn't take shit from nobody and spoke his mind. I was going to recommend this book to everybody.

Time flew by and I was at the end of the book when I noticed Jonathan getting off the highway. I saw a sign that read,

"Welcome to Chattanooga." He pulled into a gas station and I knew I had to get out to get some sweets. Katrina didn't pack a honey bun, Twinkie, or even a chocolate cupcake. I needed that shit in my life like I needed—never mind that.

The thought of sex was the last thing I wanted on my mind. It had been almost a month and I was feinin'. "Aye, Mee? Get up so you can stretch your legs. I'm going in to gets some snacks," I said nudging her awake.

It took a few seconds to realize we had stopped. Rubbing her eyes, she looked around like she was trying to figure out where we were. I knew she had no idea. I opened the door and started to get out. "Where are we?" she asked, picking her purse up from the floor of the truck.

"Girl, we are in Chattanooga, Tennessee. I guess Jonathan had to stop for gas. You have been sleeping for the last four hours. She pulled her phone out and mumbled under her breath. It was three o'clock and we still had two more hours to be cramped in the truck. I got out and walked around to Kaymee's side, waiting on her to get out.

As we walked to the entrance of the gas station, I decided to dip off to smoke. Mee knew what I was on and followed so I wouldn't be alone. Rounding the corner, there was a car parked next to the dumpster. There was a guy and a woman going at it in the front seat of a Toyota Corolla. The bitch was riding his ass like a stallion. She had her hand wrapped around his throat and his face was red as hell.

I pulled out my blunt and fired it up. This shit was better than the videos I watched on porn hub. Her titties were bouncing up and down and she didn't seem to care if they were seen or not. After hitting the blunt to the halfway point, I took out my phone and started recording them.

"Poe, don't do them like that. Put that phone away," Mee tried to whisper.

The blond-haired bitch looked over at us and smiled. She knew what the fuck was going on and she was loving every minute of it. Knowing she was being watched made her work harder for the orgasm she was seeking. She started tonguing the dude down and he was all for it until he opened his eyes and saw me with my phone in hand.

"What are you doing?" he shrieked as he pushed the woman off him.

He was struggling to pull up his pants, while opening the door. He was so worried about me recording that he forgot to put his little Vienna sausage in his pants. I started laughing on sight because the bitch had me thinking his ass was packing.

"I'm about to make yo' ass famous. How the hell are y'all fucking in a public spot and not expect anybody to see you? Man, this shit is going on the Internet and it will go viral because I have before and after footage. You may want to put the little guy away. She just catfished us all the way she was acting bouncing on air," I said, laughing.

Blondie stepped out of the car with a slinky ass dress on that barely covered her ass. She walked toward me and without any shoes on and said, "I don't give a fuck. Make me famous. Maybe I won't have to hoe no more." She was posing for the camera and then she smiled. Her teeth looked like she was fed meth instead of formula as a baby. I was praying she was as old as she looked because baby girl looked like she was kicking sixty in the ass.

"What the fuck you mean make you famous! Bitch, I got a family and I'm not losing it because of your pussy!" he screamed at her.

"You weren't thinking about that shit when I was riding your face, were you? Or when I let you fuck me in the ass with your little pecker! You paid for this shit and it wasn't the first time, so don't act like you don't know what was at stake, mutherfucker!"

The scene before me was hilarious. I kept the camera rolling and I couldn't wait to upload the shit. I felt like the cameraman of a *Cheaters* episode. I've never seen anything like this in my life. Finishing the blunt, I tossed the roach on the ground and zoomed in on both of their faces before I ended the video.

"I'm gonna let y'all work that out. Have a nice day and find somewhere else to do all that nasty shit she mentioned," I laughed, walking back around the corner.

You could hear dude screaming about how his life was about to be ruined and he blamed it all on the hoe. It was funny how he tried to make it seem as if he had nothing to do with what transpired. That's why I was good on being in a relationship. Cheating niggas came in all shapes and colors.

"Poe, you are so wrong for that, but it was pretty funny," Mee said, laughing as we entered the store.

"Girl, I couldn't' let that moment pass me by. No one would believe me if I only told the story. I needed the visual to back that shit up."

I went straight to the section with the cakes and cookies. Picking up everything I wanted, I made my way to the cooler and grabbed a couple bottles of white and chocolate milk. Mee grabbed what she wanted and we went to check out. I grabbed a couple packs of mango swishers to go with the loud I had in my purse. I wanted to be ready to smoke without having to ask about stores when we got to Atlanta.

As we got closer to the truck, Jonathan was standing with the door open on his phone. He smiled at us and ended his call. "Y'all know that shit was wrong, right?"

"What you talking about?" I said, laughing.

"That man was ready to find the nearest bridge to jump off of when he drove away from here. He could be heard screaming at that woman all the way over here. I knew y'all had something to do with it because Katrina saw y'all walk from that direction before going into the store."

"I'm gonna be real honest with you. It was me and I went to smoke. Being high as hell, I couldn't ignore it. But I felt no remorse because she tricked my ass when his lil' dude wasn't longer than my pinky toe," I said, laughing harder.

"Get in the car. We will be in Georgia in two hours or less," he said, laughing and getting in and starting up the car.

178

Back on the road, we learned some things about Georgia. It was a good thing we had the entire weekend to sightsee because come Monday, it was going to be all about getting good grades and scoping out the niggas. Two hours later, we were in Georgia. We went to a restaurant to have dinner then we were back on the road to Jonathan's house. We pulled up to a beautiful home that looked like a mini mansion.

"This you, daddy?" Kaymee asked, bouncing like a kid as Jonathan parked in the three-car garage.

"Yeah, baby girl. Let's go inside so I can show y'all around.

## Chapter 21
### Drayton

Monty and I made it to Georgia around noon and I was just waking up. I came straight to the apartment that we were able to get off campus and clunked out. Since we were Juniors, we didn't have to live in the dorms, but I was going to love the privacy that Monty and I we would have. We had a two-bedroom, two-bath, with a living room, kitchen, and a balcony. There was a pool and exercise room.

As I walked out of the bathroom, my cell rang and I picked it up off the nightstand. When I looked at the screen a guilty feeling ran through my body. "Melody" was displayed on the screen. I knew I shouldn't have answered, but I did.

"What up, ma? How you been?"

"Hey, Drayton. I'm good. I just left your dorm and you're not there. I know you didn't decide not to come back," she said into the phone.

Her voice was sexy as fuck and I actually missed hearing it. Melody was one of the many chicks that I messed around with from time to time. She and I had been doing our thing for about a year and a half, but we never put a label on what we had. All summer long she had been blowing up my phone, but I ignored her because I was all about Kaymee. I was ready to end everything with everyone to be with her.

"Nah, I'm back. I live in an apartment now. I didn't want to do the dorm thing for my last two years. I'm a grown ass man and need my own space. It's time for me to do what I have to do on my own. It's good to hear from you."

"If you had answered the phone, you would've heard from me sooner. If I didn't know any better, I would say you had me on the block list for three months. What bitch had your attention while you were gone? I sure wasn't on your mind. I didn't even get a call from you the entire time," she said with attitude.

"Hold that shit down, Mel. I'm not trying to hear all that nagging. I just got back. I'm gon' be honest, though. I did meet someone and it's serious between us. What we had is no more. I'm no longer available for our rendezvous."

I didn't want to break it to her like that, but I didn't know any other way other than to be up front. Melody was quiet for a minute but what she said hit me like a ton of bricks. "I hope whoever you're calling yourself being serious about is ready to be a step mama."

"Come again? What the fuck do that mean, Mel?"

"Just what I said. I've been calling to let you know that I'm pregnant. When we got together a month before you left, you left a little something behind. When you didn't answer, I was pissed and I went to the abortion clinic, but I couldn't go through with it. I didn't want to make that decision without telling you first."

"Look, Mel. I'm not ready to be a daddy to any damn child. You should've left a voicemail or something. For somebody that wanted to tell me something, you sure didn't try too hard to get the information to me. On top of that, how do I know that's my baby? We weren't together and I know I was doing me because I was a single muthafucka."

I knew deep down that Melody wasn't seeing another nigga while she was fucking with me because she was one of those goody girls from Alabama. I was her first and she caved to my voice whenever I said anything to her. Outside of school, the only thing she did was waited around to see what I was going to be on. She partied a little bit only because of me. Other than that, she was laid back.

"I know you are not going to try to pull that shit with me, Dray. You know that you are the only man that I've been with! That's some foul shit to say to me. Face it, we are about to be parents and there's nothing you can do about it because I'm keeping our baby," she cried into the phone.

"Are you still living in the same place?" I asked.

"Yes, but I was about to go to Walmart to pick up some food for the house."

"I'm on my way. I'll take you. Give me thirty minutes," I said, hanging up.

Dragging my hand down my face, I stared at the wall until colors started bouncing around in front of my face. This shit couldn't be happening to me. How the hell was I supposed to explain this shit to Kaymee? I don't know how long I had been sitting there but Monty's voice cut into my thoughts.

"What's going on, bro? You're looking like you lost your best friend or some shit."

"Man, fam. Shit fucked up. Do you remember Melody?"

"Melody, Melody. Oh, yeah. Shawty that's a preacher's daughter. What about her?" he asked, leaning against the wall.

"She just called and said she's been trying to contact me for months. She ain't lying because I saw every time she called up until I blocked her. I took all them hoes off the block list today and she said that she's pregnant. What the fuck am I gon' do with a baby while I'm trying to be in a relationship with Kaymee?"

My mind was all over the place with the shit Melody sprung on me. I knew I had to go over to her crib to see for myself that she was pregnant. Kaymee would be in Atlanta soon and I didn't want her to find out about Melody and the baby from anyone but me.

"Damn. You on your own with that shit, fam. If you talk to Mee about it, I think she will take it for what it is. How the relationship is gon' go afterwards, I can't call that. Being truthful is a first step, though, and then you can see where it goes from there. What are you about to do now, though?"

"I'm about to go meet up with Melody to see if she is actually pregnant and talk about how we are gon' handle this shit. Brah, how the hell did I go from winning the heart of the girl that I want to be with to becoming a damn daddy?"

"I don't' know. You need to handle that shit, though. Let me know how things go. I'm about to hit the streets and get some of this shit off. I have to meet up with Jonathan when he calls to discuss business, too. But my phone is on and ready if you need me."

"A'ight, cool. Yeah, you deal with that nigga because I don't' have shit to say to him right now."

"You gon' have to learn how to decipher between money and personal shit because ain't nothing coming before my bread. I don't know how many times I have to tell you that he wasn't wrong for coming at you the way he did. Shid, I would've been on the same shit had you talked to my daughter like that. He did what a father was supposed to do. Get off that bullshit, Dray, for real."

I wasn't trying to hear the shit that Monty was talking because I wanted to get with Jonathan's ass for the disrespect. This wasn't the time to dwell on that, though. I had bigger things to deal with at the moment and it didn't have anything to do with Jonathan. Standing from the chair that I was sitting in, I gathered my phone and keys and headed out.

Once I got in my car, my phone started ringing again. I thought for sure it was going to be Melody again but to my surprise, it was Alexis. She was one of the hoes of Spelman. Alexis had fucked every nigga at Morehouse and I had to have her. She could suck a dick like it was a thick milkshake in a straw. The bitch was book smart as well a street smart. She was one of them bitches that could change before your eyes like a chameleon. It was a wonder why she was going to school to be a lawyer.

I started fucking with her my freshman year when I met her at a frat party. She was on the dance floor looking like a chocolate goddess. Standing five foot seven, she was thick in all the right places with weave flowing down her back. She had bowed legs and a camel toe that could be seen from across the room. When I say baby girl was fly, she was fly. She was working the dance floor to a Jamaican beat and was grinding hard. I wanted her to gyrate on my dick just like that. In the end, I got what I wanted and loved every minute of it.

This was not the time to answer the call from her because I already knew what she wanted. Maybe after I left Melody, I'd call her back to break her off. Pulling up to Melody's loft, I sat there for a few seconds then got out. I was scared as hell because I didn't know how to feel. The world we lived in was something that I didn't want to bring a kid into. It was fucked up in these streets, but that's what happened when you got caught up in the heat of passion.

I walked to the door and stared at the panel of bells. When I raised my hand to press the button, the buzzer sounded indicating the door was unlocked for me to enter. Melody must've been looking out of the window and knew I was standing by the door. I pulled the door and went in, walking slowly toward the elevator.

Her loft was located at the end of the hall and I swear the short walk seemed like I was walking to the death chamber. My feet felt like lead was wearing them down and I could barely lift them with every step I took. I made it to the door and Melody was standing holding the door open for me.

"Hey," I said when I saw her. She nodded her head while stepping to the side so I could enter. My eyes focused on her tiny baby bump and I knew then, she was telling the truth. If my calculations were correct, she should've been four months along. Even if I wanted her to get an abortion, it was too late. The baby was coming if I wanted it to or not.

She had on a pair of black leggings on with a form-fitting tank that hugged her belly well. Her feet were tiny and cute like I remembered and she was glowing. The time we spent together was always fun and we had good times. I just wasn't ready to settle down at the moment. I wouldn't lie, though. She was first in line to be my woman until I met Kaymee.

"How have you been, Mel?" I asked, sitting on the stool to her island counter.

"I've been dealing with this pregnancy alone, so that has been a strain on me. Even though I am twenty-four years old, my parents don't agree with me having a baby out of wedlock.

They are worried about what the congregation at the church will say."

She had a sad look on her face and it looked like she was going to cry. I felt bad because I knew how her parents were when it came to her. They wanted her to live her life as a nun and that life wasn't for everyone. Melody is from Alabama and was raised in the church. When she met me, her sex drive went from nonexistent to overload. I wasn't complaining because I was able to mold her into what I wanted her to be.

"Fuck what they think! Don't cry over that shit. I see the look in your eyes. We will have to do what needs to be done to take care of our baby. Their whole congregation is sinning all day every day except on Sunday, so they don't have room to judge no damn body. If they don't want to have anything to do with you, I'm gon' step up and help you out regardless."

"Dray, I hope you mean what you are saying. I don't want any drama with your girlfriend. What I'm not trying to be is a secret baby mama. I'm going to need you to tell your girl about the baby. If she means anything to you, be up straight with her. Don't let her find out in a way that will hurt her."

I felt what she was saying and I didn't think I needed to tell Kaymee about this situation right away. I was still kind of upset with her for what happened between her dad and I. She didn't know I left Chicago and I didn't attempt to reach out to inform her either. My anger was the reason for the way I was looking at Melody at that moment.

Not only was she looking good standing in front of me, but she was carrying my baby. I didn't think about what I did next, I grabbed Melody around her waist and moved her closer and between my legs. Rubbing her stomach, I lifted her shirt and planted a couple kisses on it. Seeing that Melody was pregnant with my own eyes had me excited about the life I helped create.

Stepping away from my affection, Melody looked at me sadly. "Dray, we have a baby on the way, but I will not tolerate any physical interactions between the two of us. The main focal point of our relationship is the baby. I will keep you posted on doctor appointments and anything else that has to do with this pregnancy. Everything else will have to be based on the friendship that we have. Crossing the lines as if we are an item is something that won't happen."

"Mel, I was only trying to show my baby some love. There's nothing wrong with letting my baby know that I will be here for him or her. I didn't mean to make you uncomfortable. I don't want you to focus on my relationship. Let me deal with that. I'm going to be here for you every step of the way throughout this pregnancy, so get ready to have me around all the time," I said, standing up from the stool.

Towering over Melody's small frame, I looked down at her and she was avoiding my eyes. I used my finger to lift her head so she was staring at me. My head lowered and my lips connected with hers. When she didn't pull away, I deepened the kiss and pushed her into my erection. We kissed for a few minutes before she pulled back and walked to the door.

"I have a doctor's appointment Tuesday morning at eight in the morning. I'll send you the address and you can meet me there. Until then, I need to go get something to cook. Are you ready to take me to the store?" I forgot she needed to go to the store, but I was a man of my word. Nodding my head, I walked to the door and held it open for her.

After taking Melody to the store, I carried the groceries that I purchased into her place and told her I would check on her later. I went to the missed calls in my phone as I sat in my car and my thumb loomed over Alexis's name. When I was about to press the call icon by her name, my phone started ringing. Kaymee was calling and I let the call go to voicemail. I wasn't ready to talk to her yet.

I went through with calling Alexis and she answered on the first ring. Her voice was so soft and sultry, my dick bricked up instantly. "Hey, boo. Long time no see. How you been?" she asked sexily.

The voice inside my head was telling me to come up with an excuse to call her back, but my libido had a mind of its own.

I didn't have to coach Lexi on anything sexual and I knew that I would be able to go as far and deep as I desired. That was something I was not about to pass up.

"I've been good. I was handling business when you called, but I'm free now. What's up?"

"Well, I want to see you. Is it possible?"

"Anything is possible, baby. Are you in the same dorm this semester?" I asked, starting my car.

"Yes, but my roomie is here. I was thinking we could get a room or something. The things I have in mind needs a bit more privacy. Mama wants to get really nasty for you, Dray."

"You know I like nasty. I'll be there in fifteen. Be ready and pack a bag, there will be no going home for either of us tonight. Is that okay with you?"

"Hell yeah, bring that D where it belongs, baby," she said ending the call.

I didn't have to worry about going home to pack a bag. I never unpacked my luggage when we got in, so I was good on that. I made my way in the direction of Spelman campus and I was ready. I thought I was ready to tell these females that I was done and be with only Kaymee, but I guess being back in Atlanta was far different from being in Chicago. I had all my bitches in arm's length and it was hard to change what I was accustomed to. This would be something I would have to work very hard to stop doing.

When I was five minutes away, I texted Lexi letting her know I would be pulling up soon. Lexi was standing outside the gate when I pulled up. She had on a pair of shorts that were cuffing her ass cheeks. The shirt that she had on showed off her toned stomach and hugged her breast. Her nipples protruded through the thin material. The way she sauntered to the car had me mesmerized. There was a slight breeze in the air that made her long hair blow in the wind, making her look even sexier to me.

She opened the door and lifted her leg to get in and her entire left ass cheek was in my face. I knew she did that purposely, but I wasn't mad at her attempt to seduce me. It worked like a charm and I had plans for her.

"Get yo' fine ass in this car and stop playing. You gon' fuck around and get pinned up in the backseat if you keep playing," I said, licking my lips.

"Boy, please. You won't be having sex with me in this damn car," she giggled as she closed the door and snapped the seatbelt in place.

Putting the car in drive, I headed to the Ramada Plaza and it took less than five minutes to get there. Grabbing Alexis's bag, I went to the trunk to get my gym bag and led the way to the entrance of the hotel. As I approached the front desk, there was a chick that I had fucked with a while back sitting behind the counter. When she saw me, her face scrunched up but she didn't act stupid.

"May I help you?" she asked with attitude.

"Yeah, let me get a room for two nights." The smile that appeared on Alexis's face told me that she was happy to spend the next couple of days with me. I wanted to give her time with me because this was going to be the last go 'round. She was getting cut the fuck off, so I had to hit her for old times' sake before I sent her on her way.

"That will be one hundred eighty-three dollars and sixty-seven cents. You would need to use a credit card or a debit card," she said, smirking at me.

This bitch must've thought I was one of these broke niggas or a baller nigga that didn't know the importance of having a credit card. I looked at her long and hard before I took my wallet out of my pocket. Handing her my card, I smirked back at her stupid ass and waited for her to swipe my shit and give it back. She was mad as hell because she thought I wasn't going to be able to produce that shit.

Slapping my card on the counter along with my receipt, she leaned over and grabbed the room keys, placing them on top of the receipt. You're in room nine zero six. Enjoy your stay at Ramada Plaza," she said, rolling her eyes.

"Thank you and have a nice night," I said snidely.

Heading to the elevator, Alexis started laughing out of nowhere. I looked at her like she was crazy because I didn't know what her problem was. "What's so funny?" I asked as I pushed the up button on the wall.

"You fucked her, didn't you?"

"Who are you talking about, girl?"

"The bitch at the front desk. She was big mad when she saw us walk in and she was rude as hell. I know you had something going on with her because you didn't snap on her for the way she was acting. It doesn't matter to me, though. You can be married with kids and I'll still swallow ya dick whole like an anaconda."

The elevator doors opened and we stepped in. Before the doors closed good, she freed my lil' man, dropped to her knees, and swallowed his ass just like she said she would. I knew then that the next two days were about to be mind-blowing. Kaymee wasn't even on my mind and all thoughts of Melody and the baby were shoved to the back until further notice.

## Chapter 22
**Kaymee**

I had been in Atlanta since Friday, it was now Sunday, and I hadn't heard from Dray at all. Every time I called, the phone rang until the voicemail picked up. After a while, it went straight to voicemail. I knew he was upset about what happened but damn, did that mean ignore the fuck out of me? I put on a happy face so my daddy and Poe didn't know what I was going through, but the shit hurt like hell.

Dray showed me that I meant everything to him in Chicago. Now that we are in Atlanta, he was nowhere to be found. I knew he was back here because Monty called me to see how I was doing. He wanted to know if Poetry and I were going to the prayer service that was held every Sunday. I talked it over with Poetry and she agreed to go because she wanted to experience everything associated with school.

My daddy began to teach me how to drive in his BMW and I was getting the hang of it. He told me once I learned how to drive, he was going to buy me a smaller car. I was glad because I didn't think I could handle that big ass truck that he bought me. Poetry lucked up though because he gave her the truck as a graduation gift. I was happy for her because she had been the one that drove it anyway.

"Kaymee, I don't really want to go to this prayer service. Do you think it would be wrong to wait until the block party starts, then we head out?" Poetry asked.

"I'm down with that. I didn't want to go either. I don't need to listen to a service to know my God. He knows my heart."

I was laying in my bed sulking, but I straightened my face when she entered. The room that I had at my daddy's house was bigger than the room I had when I was living with Dot. Hell, the closet was bigger than my old room to tell the truth.

There were six bedrooms, four bathrooms, a kitchen, a living room, a full basement, and an exercise room. The circular driveway was beautiful and it had a three-car garage. The backyard was huge. There was a swimming pool, a deck, and a pool house in the back as well as a basketball court. I dreamt about living in a home like this all my life. Now that my daddy was back in my life, I somewhat had it.

Poetry crawled in my king-sized bed and laid down beside me. She sat back up and looked at me strangely. "Mee, please tell me the wetness on that pillow is not snot."

I laughed and shook my head no. "It's not snot. I was crying because Dray is still not answering my calls. I knew he was mad at me but it's been four days and he still hasn't answered when I called. He didn't seem like the kind of guy that would wine and dine me, take my virginity and leave. The incident didn't warrant him to just stop talking to me at a drop of a dime. He treated me like a queen back in Chicago. Now it seems like I meant nothing to him."

A fresh set of tears fell from my eyes and there was nothing I could do to stop them from flowing. My heart was hurting so badly. I loved Dray even though I've only known him for three months. The way he made me feel in and out of the bedroom was a case of love I'd never experienced before. I didn't know what I was going to do about the way I felt.

"Kaymee, I don't want to see you crying over him. If he wants to act like an asshole, let him do him. God didn't stop making men when they made his black ass. Dry those tears and go in that closet and find something to wear that's gonna turn every nigga head that you pass. We are bound to see his ass at the block party later."

"Poe, I don't want to get the attention of anyone else. I want Dray to tell me what's going on, then maybe we can get back on track. You know, get back to loving each other the way we were back home."

"You can't force a man to talk to you. Chicago is your territory, but Atlanta is his. I hate to say this, but there is no telling what Dray has going on here. We don't know what's been going on in the past. I don't want to use this as an example, but I

192

have to. Monty was doing all types of bullshit down here that I didn't know about. Dray could be on the same shit."

"Dray wouldn't do that to me, Poe. I asked him if he had anyone that he was seeing and he said he wasn't. I believe him. I think he's just still mad at me."

"I know that this is your first relationship and all, but I refuse to let you lay here and be gullible. The signs are there and I want you to open your eyes to the 'what if'. Don't give Dray the benefit of the doubt without knowing the facts. Deep down, I feel like he has been laid up. I wouldn't be surprised if his skeletons start falling out of his closet like an avalanche, but I will have my shoulder ready for you to cry on. Then we are going out to celebrate."

"I'm not going to sit here and let you bash him like that, Poe. That's not right, so don't do that. We don't know what's going on with him. I will find out what the problem is when I finally talk to him."

"Okay, I will stop taking about *your* problem with Dray. I'm sorry that it's a sensitive subject for you to know that this nigga is dirty. I love you like a sister and I'm not trying to upset you. I'm on the outside looking in and I can see what's going on. Time will tell what he does when you're not in his presence," she said, getting up. "I'll leave you alone to think about what I said. We can leave about four o'clock to go to the block party. I love you, sis."

Poetry left me with a lot to think about, but. I didn't want to believe that Dray was cheating on me. He promised he wouldn't hurt me. I laid in the bed and cried as I continuously called his phone without getting an answer. It didn't go to voicemail, so he saw every time I called. He just didn't answer.

I decided to call Monty to see if he had talked to Dray. Listening to the phone ringing, I was about to end the call when he answered. I heard the sounds of clapping and singing in the background.

"Mee, where y'all at?" he asked.

"Have you seen Dray in the last four days? I haven't talked to him since we were in Chicago."

He didn't say anything for a minute or so. After a while the music started fading in the background. I didn't know what Monty was doing but I heard rustling in the phone before he spoke again.

"What do you mean you haven't talked to him?"

"I've been calling him and he has yet to pick up his phone for me. Tell me what's going on, bro. I know you are not covering for him over me."

"Ain't no way I'm taking any muthafuckas side over yours. I don't know what's going on with Dray, but he is okay. I've seen him, but I didn't know he hadn't talked to you in all that time. When I see him, I will tell him to give you a call. When will y'all be heading this way?"

"We will be out for the block party. We decided not to go to the prayer service."

"Alright, call me when y'all are on your way. I'll see y'all later. Tell Poetry I love her," he said, ending the call.

I decide to go back to sleep before we got ready for the block party. I heard that the parties down south be off the hook. The way I was feeling about Dray was not going to stop me from enjoying myself. We were going to party like it was nineteen ninety-nine in Georgia. Turning over fluffing my pillow, I closed my eyes and fell asleep.

\*\*\*

Poetry came barging in my room waking me with her music bumping like she was at the club. I looked up at her and she was twerking in a pair of white capris with an off the shoulder red top. The red sandals that she had on showed off her pretty toes that were freshly manicured. Her hair was flowing down her back, bone straight with a part down the middle. She didn't have on any makeup and she was still beautiful.

"Poe, what's your problem and why are you bouncing around like you in a music video?"

"Girl, I'm ready to go to this block party and turn the fuck up! Get out of that bed so we can leave. It's time for us to see what we can get into down here in Georgia."

Getting out of the bed, I went to my closet and searched for something to wear for the day. I decided to wear a green maxi dress and a pair of green and white sandals. I bought the dress when we went to the mall back home and today is the first time I would wear it.

"Let me take a shower and get dressed. I have to get pretty," I said, walking to the bathroom door. Turning around to face Poe, I said, "Thank you for always being there when I need you. You have always had my back and I'm sorry that I wasn't trying to hear what you were saying about Dray. I want to hear from him why he has been ignoring me. I know you were only trying to look out for me. Until I learn the truth, I will give him the benefit of the doubt. I don't want you to be mad at me, nor do I want you to think of me as a stupid weak chick."

"Kaymee, I will never call you any of those things. Life has a way of taking you through things to make you stronger. I'm not in the position to throw stones at you. My life is not peachy if you haven't noticed. You have to walk the path of life the way you feel fit. I will be here for you either way."

"Enough of this mushy shit, let me get ready so we can get out of here," I said, stepping in the bathroom and closing the door.

I stepped out of the bathroom after about twenty minutes and as I entered the room, Poetry looked up from her phone and smiled big. She jumped up from the bed and started dancing around swinging her arms above her head. She let out a scream that almost pierced my eardrums.

"Bitch! You are wearing the fuck out of that dress! What did you do to your hair? I love it!"

"Why are you acting like I usually dress like a bum? I always look good when I go out."

"Nah, bestie. There is something different about you on this here day. You got your grown woman thang going on. I don't know. It seems as if you're going out to prove a point. Yo' ass is fine!"

"Awww, thank you so much. Give me a minute. I have to do my makeup to make this look pop. As far as my hair, all I did was twist the hair on the sides and brought them together in a fishtail to the back. I wanted my hair off my face today."

"You definitely did that! Hurry up! We need to go so you can be seen!"

There was a knock on the door and my daddy walked in looking all handsome and stuff. "Hey, babies. Where are you guys off to?" he asked.

"We are going to the block party on campus," I said, while placing my makeup case on the dresser.

"I want you two to be careful. This is not Chicago, but there are still crazy muthafuckas down here, too. The hood is not far from the college, so don't trust anyone. If y'all need me at any time, call me!" he barked. "That includes Dray's ass, too, Kaymee."

"Daddy, Dray is not the one you have to worry about. But I will call you if I need to, I promise," I said, adding the green eye shadow to my eyelids on top of the smoky grey color I applied first. I lined my eyes with black eyeliner and glossed my lips with a nude lip gloss. I was ready to step out looking like the diva I was born to be.

"You look beautiful, baby. Have fun and call me if y'all are not coming back here tonight."

"Thank you, daddy. We will be back because you have to help us move into the dorm tomorrow," I said.

"Isn't that what those two niggas y'all call your boyfriends are for?" Both of us rolled our eyes without responding. "I guess that's a no," he said, laughing. "Well, I'll see y'all later.

I love y'all." He kissed me on my cheek and hugged Poe before he left out of my room.

When the door closed behind my dad, I glanced at my best friend. The expression on her face showed signs of sadness. She blinked rapidly as if she was fighting back tears. Jonathan mentioning our boyfriends is what brought her mood on.

"He told me to tell you he loves you, Poe."

"I don't care about anything Monty has to say. There was something in my eye," she said, pulling on her eyelid. "Okay, that's better. My vision was out of focus for a minute, but I'm good now. You ready to go see what this party is about?"

"Yeah, let's do this," I said grabbing my phone.

My dad lived twenty minutes from campus and when we pulled into the parking lot, it was lit. There were people everywhere because the event was being held at Morehouse but the students from Spelman and Clark were in attendance, as well. I could tell that it was going to be hard not to party every weekend around there. The discipline of self was going to have to come full force because it was going to be easy getting sucked in with the events I was sure were coming.

"Girl, look at this shit. This place is live!" Poe screamed, looking around.

I was texting Monty, letting him know we were in the student center parking lot. Once I told him, he said he was already out there and to come to the back where he was. I didn't let Poe know that I was texting him. I just gave her directions.

"Sis, let's park in the back closer to the other exit. There aren't too many cars on that end," I said, pointing in the direction I wanted her to go.

"I'm with you there. I'm not trying to be waiting long to get out of this bitch when it's time to roll out."

When she turned down the back row, that's when we saw Monty standing with a cup in his hand with a slew of people. I could feel Poe's eyes on me, but she didn't say anything. She parked a couple cars down and I noticed Monty coming our way.

"Don't look now, but bro is coming," I said to her.

"You knew this shit already, but I'm gonna play nice this time. Don't set me up again, Mee. This isn't going to change anything between us. I'm still not going back to him."

Before I could respond, he was on her side of the truck, checking her out. "Y'all looking good," he said, smiling. "Hey, Poe. How you been?" he asked.

"I'm alright, Montez and yourself?"

"I can't complain. Mee! What's up, baby girl? You gon' start back hangin' with ya boy soon? Yo' ass kind of cut a nigga off when ya girl did. We can still hang out sometime," he said, laughing.

"It's not like that, bro. You know I love you," I said, getting out of the truck.

Poetry didn't attempt to open her door because Monty was ogling her and she couldn't. He looked so cute, but you could tell by the bags under his eyes that he hadn't been sleeping well. At least he had a sparkle in his eye that day, along with a smile.

"Would you step back so I can get out?" she asked nicely.

"Oh, my bad. Let the windows up before you get out, though. I don't need nobody trying no funny shit," he said, stepping back a few feet to allow her to open the door.

She inserted the key and let the windows up before stepping out. Looking everywhere but at Montez, Poetry started walking across the parking lot. I knew it was hard for her to see past the deception, but I was trying to catch up with bro.

"Damn, she's never gonna forgive me for that shit, huh? I miss her ass like crazy, Mee." He was watching her walk away like a sick puppy.

"Give her time. She's always saying that she doesn't hate you, she just can't be with you."

"She has every right to think that way. I just want her back in my life and I will find a way to get her."

"Where's ya boy, Monty?"

"Dray is out here somewhere. He was over there chilling with us right before you texted saying you were here. I don't know where he went, though. He told me what happened and I told him that he needed to apologize to you. That hasn't happened, I'm assuming."

"No, I still haven't talked to him. Every time I call, I get his voicemail."

"Stop sweating him. Keep your focus on school and not on Dray. Let's walk and see what's going on around here. You will see how we party down here in Hotlanta," he said, laughing.

Many of the women were dressed like strippers. I knew it was hot, but that didn't mean walk around with your draws on. There had to be a lot of random fucking taking place on all three campuses. As we walked to the front of the building where I found out there will be a concert later, Poetry was rushing our way. Monty immediately started walking faster to make it to her.

When she was within earshot, she started yelling. "Is this what y'all do here in Atlanta, Montez?" she asked, stopping in front of us.

"What are you talking about, Poe? I'm out here having a good time, that's all."

"I'm gonna show you what I'm talking about. Mee, brace yourself because you are not gonna like what you are about to see," she said, leading the way to the back of a building.

As soon as we saw a group of people dancing and got closer, I could see Dray dancing in the middle of the circle with a woman that was topless. Her legs were wrapped around his waist and she was gyrating on his dick. Using his neck as support, she placed her feet on the ground and turned her back on him. The skirt she had on rose above her ass cheeks and Dray's hands were all over them.

The beat dropped and she went hard, popping her ass. Dray had the nerve to move her thong to the side, getting an eyeful of her pussy from the back. This chick was enjoying every bit of what was going on because she didn't stop when he rubbed his thumb down her ass crack. Turning around, she embraced him in a hug and kissed his lips. Instead of pulling away, he deepened the kiss while palming her ass. The kiss was an intimate one. Their tongues were tangled together like they were familiar with one another.

"Dray! What the fuck is going on?" I yelled, moving forward.

He broke the kiss and stepped back from the woman. The crowd was going crazy for the drama that was bound to take place. Standing with his mouth open, he moved toward me but was pulled back by the woman he was entertaining.

"I know damn well you are not fucking with another bitch! Not after the last couple of days we just had. Dray what happened to, 'it's me and you forever'?" she asked, while still holding his arm.

*To Be Continued...*
Love Shouldn't Hurt 3
Coming Soon

## Submission Guideline.

Submit the first three chapters of your completed manuscript to ldpsubmissions@gmail.com, subject line: Your book's title. The manuscript must be in a .doc file and sent as an attachment. Document should be in Times New Roman, double spaced and in size 12 font. Also, provide your synopsis and full contact information. If sending multiple submissions, they must each be in a separate email.

Have a story but no way to send it electronically? You can still submit to LDP/Ca$h Presents. Send in the first three chapters, written or typed, of your completed manuscript to:

LDP: Submissions Dept
Po Box 870494
Mesquite, Tx 75187

*DO NOT send original manuscript. Must be a duplicate.*

Provide your synopsis and a cover letter containing your full contact information.

Thanks for considering LDP and Ca$h Presents.

# Meesha

# Love Shouldn't Hurt 2

By **Mimi**

WHAT BAD BITCHES DO **III**

By **Aryanna**

THE COST OF LOYALTY **II**

By **Kweli**

SHE FELL IN LOVE WITH A REAL ONE **II**

By **Tamara Butler**

LOVE SHOULDN'T HURT **III**

By **Meesha**

CORRUPTED BY A GANGSTA **III**

By **Destiny Skai**

A GANGSTER'S CODE II

By **J-Blunt**

KING OF NEW YORK II

By **T.J. Edwards**

CUM FOR ME **IV**

By **Ca$h & Company**

STEADY MOBBN' 2

By **Marcellus Allen**


**Available Now**

RESTRAINING ORDER **I & II**

By **CA$H & Coffee**

LOVE KNOWS NO BOUNDARIES **I II & III**

By **Coffee**

RAISED AS A GOON I, II, III & IV

BRED BY THE SLUMS I, II, III

BLAST FOR ME I & II

By **Ghost**

Meesha

LAY IT DOWN **I & II**
LAST OF A DYING BREED
BLOOD STAINS OF A SHOTTA I & II
By **Jamaica**
LOYAL TO THE GAME
LOYAL TO THE GAME II
LOYAL TO THE GAME III
By **TJ & Jelissa**
BLOODY COMMAS I & II
SKI MASK CARTEL I  II & III
KING OF NEW YORK
By **T.J. Edwards**
IF LOVING HIM IS WRONG…I & II
By **Jelissa**
WHEN THE STREETS CLAP BACK I & II III
By **Jibril Williams**
A DISTINGUISHED THUG STOLE MY HEART I II & III
LOVE SHOULDN'T HURT I II
By **Meesha**
A GANGSTER'S CODE
**By J-Blunt**
PUSH IT TO THE LIMIT
By **Bre' Hayes**
BLOOD OF A BOSS **I, II, III & IV**
By **Askari**
THE STREETS BLEED MURDER **I, II & III**
THE HEART OF A GANGSTA I II& III
By **Jerry Jackson**
CUM FOR ME
CUM FOR ME 2

204

CUM FOR ME 3

An **LDP Erotica Collaboration**

BRIDE OF A HUSTLA **I  II & II**

THE FETTI GIRLS **I, II& III**

CORRUPTED BY A GANGSTA I & II

By **Destiny Skai**

WHEN A GOOD GIRL GOES BAD

By **Adrienne**

A GANGSTER'S REVENGE **I II III & IV**

THE BOSS MAN'S DAUGHTERS

THE BOSS MAN'S DAUGHTERS II

THE BOSSMAN'S DAUGHTERS III

THE BOSSMAN'S DAUGHTERS IV

THE BOSS MAN'S DAUGHTERS **V**

A SAVAGE LOVE  **I & II**

BAE BELONGS TO ME

A HUSTLER'S DECEIT I, II

WHAT BAD BITCHES DO I, II

By **Aryanna**

A KINGPIN'S AMBITON

A KINGPIN'S AMBITION **II**

I MURDER FOR THE DOUGH

By **Ambitious**

TRUE SAVAGE

TRUE SAVAGE II

TRUE SAVAGE **III**

TRUE SAVAGE **IV**

By **Chris Green**

A DOPEBOY'S PRAYER

By **Eddie "Wolf" Lee**

Meesha

THE KING CARTEL **I, II & III**
By **Frank Gresham**
THESE NIGGAS AIN'T LOYAL **I, II & III**
By **Nikki Tee**
GANGSTA SHYT **I II &III**
By **CATO**
THE ULTIMATE BETRAYAL
By **Phoenix**
BOSS'N UP **I , II & III**
By **Royal Nicole**
I LOVE YOU TO DEATH
**By Destiny J**
I RIDE FOR MY HITTA
I STILL RIDE FOR MY HITTA
By **Misty Holt**
LOVE & CHASIN' PAPER
By **Qay Crockett**
TO DIE IN VAIN
By **ASAD**
BROOKLYN HUSTLAZ
By **Boogsy Morina**
BROOKLYN ON LOCK I & II
By **Sonovia**
GANGSTA CITY
By **Teddy Duke**
A DRUG KING AND HIS DIAMOND I & II
A DOPEMAN'S RICHES
**By Nicole Goosby**
TRAPHOUSE KING I & II
By **Hood Rich**